Operation Palmetto

By

R.T. Breach

Operation Palmetto by R.T. Breach

Published by Covert Publishing House
Dallas, GA 30132

https://rtbreach.com

For permissions, contact:

rtb@rtbreach.com

Cover by Covertwebman

Editing by Sandra Haven and Steve Anderson.

ISBN: 978-1-7363786-1-8

Dedicated to those among us who risk it all in the line of duty.

I

Monday, April 8, 10:30 pm, Nuremberg, Germany

Dr. Vahan Nafisi looked himself over in the mirror, straightening his tie. He took a deep breath, exhaling as he folded a paper towel and slid it into his pocket. Many lies had passed from his lips, eventually landing him at this point. The guilt enough that it made him mutter a prayer of forgiveness as he exited the men's room.

Soft piano music and the murmur of voices enveloped him upon returning to the highbrow gala. Attendees comprised scientists from around the world in a chandelier-lit dining hall. Dozens of guests stood at high-top tables, glasses of champagne or wine in hand. They chatted, smiled, and laughed at each other's jokes. Everybody seemed so carefree.

It poisoned Vahan with envy. Eyes darting around the elegant room, he turned and hurried toward the side that he suspected housed a secondary exit.

Having to sneak away like this seems so cowardly. Like they're actual scientists, and I am just an overly religious sucker.

From the corner of his eye, Vahan noticed a man's head following his passing. Though he tried staying relaxed, he couldn't help breathing heavily. The sound of it seemed loud enough to draw the everyone's attention. To his relief, the man eyeing him turned back to his date across the little table.

A drop of sweat crawled from the top of Vahan's bald head and coursed down his temple. Picking up his pace, he swiped his head with the paper towel from his pocket and glanced over his shoulder. Nobody paid any attention to him at all. *Relax, Vahan, you're paranoid. Just stay calm. They haven't followed you. They don't have any idea you are not going back home. Just get out of here, get to the airport, and get to your brother.*

Born and raised in Iran, he'd always loved his country. But here he stood, in Nuremberg, Germany, doing the unthinkable—running away. It was fun and games until his friends got murdered.

Vahan lived with government stooges keeping tabs on him all day for years back home. Ever since he'd taken a science position at the Natanz nuclear facility, they'd become as ubiquitous as the family pet. If one lives that long with Revolutionary Guard soldiers watching ones every move, one acclimated to constant oversight. Right now, he felt alone, exposed, and out of place.

When he started at Natanz, he knew there'd be risks. He'd thought the worst would be radiation. As it turned out, Israeli assassins were deadlier than charged particles. Much deadlier. Motorcycle-riding thugs used magnetic bombs placed on the side of cars while in motion, murdering his colleagues as they commuted. They were his friends, too.

Vahan shuddered thinking of their fate and the family's grief. Fleeing your home land, where one lived and worked all their life, was something few people planned. Doubtless not Vahan with his conservative outlook on life. Yet, as if sent from Allah, a letter arrived the day after the second murder, inviting him to this conference. Which meant a ticket out of Iran and the madness.

If my wife and children were still alive, I would stay. But there is nobody there for me anymore. My closest friends are dead now. All I have in the world is my brother, Hedyeh.

He found a corridor leading out of the main dining hall and peered toward its windowless end. On a hunch, he figured an exit must be at the end to avoid any fire safety hazard. He pulled out his phone and glanced around, pretending answer the a call while moving into the corridor.

To one side, behind dark curtains, he saw the seam of a door. A quick peek behind revealed an emergency exit. At the opposite end of this hallway, where it emptied into the dining hall, he saw a pair of men scanning the room.

Surly government minders always peered over his shoulder back home. Vahan knew the face of Quds Force agents when he saw them. Iran's secret police were barely thirty meters away. Before they noticed him, he slipped through the exit door. The sound of it latching closed behind made his heart skip a beat.

It clicked so loudly. They must be looking for me. You've done it, Vahan; you're committed now. Maybe they'll not follow from this point on if I hurry. By the look of them, they hadn't spied me yet. Run!

Ten meters down the short, dull-white utility passage stood another door. A blue sign was centered on it with a stickman standing on white zigzagging lines. Vahan yanked it open and hustled down five flights. When he reached the bottom, he didn't pause before bursting out the exit door.

It opened onto a two-by-two-meter landing with a short set of stairs leading down into a dimly lit narrow alley. When the door slammed, he stopped on the stairs and glared back, holding a hand to his hammering sixty-one-year-old heart.

I haven't moved that fast in a while. If they find me after that, then I give up. I think, by the time they figure it out, this out-of-shape old fox will have given them the slip.

He spun back around and hurried along the alley until he skidded to a stop on a sidewalk. Looking left, he scanned the cars cruising past. He frantically waved at the nearest taxi. The driver waved back and moved to pull over. Feeling unprotected, Vahan stepped back from the curb, sidling up close to the building, awaiting for the cab.

Early spring evenings were still crisp. He flipped up his collar; the chill in the air meant he didn't appear out-of-place doing it. The taxi stopped at the curb. He took three steps and practically dove for the rear-door handle.

As he slid onto the seat, he said in broken German, "I'd like to go to the airport, please."

"Nuremberg International?" the driver asked, glancing into the rearview mirror.

Not expecting multiple choices, Vahan hesitated—no time to dig out his phone and check the airline's app. Getting away clean was priority one. Even if he wound up at the wrong airport, it would be miles from here and those thugs.

"Uh, yes, the big one. International flights."

After pecking at his dash-mounted navigation device, the driver said over his shoulder, "GPS says it'll be twelve minutes, sir."

"Okay, that is fine."

The taxi moved into traffic.

He'd watched out the back window as they accelerated away. To his horror, the two men from the gala emerged from the alley he'd vacated. They stopped at the curb where he'd been standing only moments earlier. They were looking for someone or something. It could only be him. He ducked out of sight.

"Sir, are you okay? Please don't get sick in my car. If you are going to be sick, I will stop or take you to a hospital."

"No, no. I'm fine. My... shoelace untied is all."

The man didn't know his shoes had no laces. Mollified, the driver gave a quick nod and continued the trip. Vahan hoped they hadn't seen him get in the taxi. When he rose, they were out of sight, several blocks behind.

I've done it! I've lost them, and soon I will be where they will never catch me. Please guide me, Allah. Please show me the way.

Initially, he'd thought to stay in Germany. When he found their asylum plans uninviting, he turned to America and his brother, who had begged him come live there. Vahan detested America and its hedonism. Hedyeh seemed to do well, though, starting a business and living comfortably. Even attending mosque regularly.

Arriving at the departure drop-off area, Vahan paid the driver, got out of the taxi, and hurried inside. He checked into his flight, jumped through the security hoops, and found a deserted set of chairs to sit by himself. His confidence grew now that he'd sheltered behind the curtain of airport security.

Yet, for the next hour, he gave sidelong looks at everyone passing through the corridor where he awaited his flight. Harried parents with fussy children, distracted business travelers, and people heading for vacations. Everything natural. His blood pressure gradually lowered.

Find me in this labyrinth if you can! Ha! This cloak-and-dagger business isn't so hard. I don't know why I was so worried.

He wouldn't consider himself genuinely safe until the plane backed away from the terminal. It would be a long night of transit before he reached his destination: Charleston, South Carolina, America. He knew that when he got there, he couldn't go straight to his brother's house. Hedyeh had feared revealing too much information in a letter, his home address in particular. They agreed via Skype—Vahan would travel to Charleston around this time, contacting his brother when he arrived.

The Quds Force men never appeared in the terminal, nor did they board the flight. Hopeful but cautious, he slept little on the plane. His mind wouldn't settle down enough for slumber. Thoughts of the future kept him awake. *They might still follow me.*

He didn't want to endanger his brother and his family. But it's America, the land of freedom and lots of guns. Fortunately, Iran had little influence over there. They couldn't operate in the open. Besides, he's a minor player, or so he saw himself. In reality, he'd been in line for promotion after a couple of colleagues vacated their positions by getting blown up. *That's probably why the Israelis hadn't killed me, too—I wasn't that important.*

Vahan didn't know that the Israelis merely missed their target when they tried assassinating him. Ignorance being bliss, all that mattered now was he's free. Quds Force, nuclear weapons, and Iran were behind him. *Thank you, Allah, for your blessing.*

II

Wednesday, April 10, 4 am, Nuremberg, Germany

Karl Gruben took one last drag off his cigarette, flicking it away afterward. Convertible cars make that convenient. He dropped his VW Eos into second gear, ready to whip a quick right into Nuremberg Airport's multi-level parking deck.

Karl and his girlfriend, Gabriella, lived in an apartment, which meant no yard for their dogs to use and early morning dog walks for him. It also made a convenient time and place to scoop dead drops. Mossad operatives left them in the form of a fake dog poop log. It unscrewed in the middle. A note tucked inside today's turd said he had a new assignment. He's to meet his handler, Hiram Roth, at 4:00 a.m. the following morning.

A meeting at the airport means one thing: I'm leaving town. I wonder where I'm going this time? Hopefully not for a long stint.

He spiraled up through the parking deck a couple of levels and found an open parking space. Once the convertible top latched into place, he got out, locked it, and walked to the stairs. Rather than go down to the terminal, he went up two more levels.

Though his job required extensive travel, he traveled light. His personal effects got confiscated upon his departure for a mission, anyway. All he had on himself right now were his cell phone, wallet, mini multi-tool knife, wristwatch, Ray-Bans, cigarettes, lighter, and car keys.

He emerged from the stairwell on the fifth level. There were fewer cars up here. The only vehicle that concerned him sat in the twelfth parking space—an old white Fiat sedan. When the driver noticed him, he stuck a hand out the window and waved him over. Without acknowledging the wave, Karl strolled toward the Fiat.

An operative could never be too careful, particularly when they were home. There's the possibility of observation by enemy spies and people you know on a personal level, too. It'd throw his rhythm off and negatively affect the mission if his girlfriend were to catch him playing spy games like a mom interrupting a boy in the middle of a Star Wars action figure adventure.

She's aware of his employment with the Israeli Institute for Intelligence and Special Operations.

After her vetting phase, they found Gabby to be a safe love interest. Karl received permission to divulge his occupation to her. It didn't sit right with his conscience deceiving her. And the Mossad isn't naïve. They know people will talk. It's inevitable. National security trumps their relationship any day of the week, though.

A good operative appeared to be nothing out of the ordinary. But spy craft came off as goofy or paranoid to the untrained eye. Some of the security measures, combined with cloak-and-dagger-style antics, might appear comical to an outsider. Unfortunately, it is an all too real life of danger and paranoia. Israel's enemies are many, and their friends few.

Karl pulled his phone from a pants pocket and pretended to be engrossed in its miraculous little screen. It isn't a busy time of day. There aren't many people around. He scanned his surroundings as he walked.

Nothing suspicious.

Sliding the phone back into his pocket, he stole another glance around as he approached.

Double check the duress signal.

As he passed the Fiat's back bumper, he peered between it and an adjacent Mercedes. On the side of the Fiat driver's door, he saw a rectangular magnetic sign stuck there. It read EcoTaxi in blue letters on a white background. *There's the sign.* Had the sign been absent, that would've signaled a wave-off.

Karl about-faced and turned into the passenger side aisle. Without a further look around, he snatched open the rear door and slid into the car's back seat. The chubby driver, who had been fiddling around on his phone, looked at Karl in the rearview mirror. They made eye contact for a moment.

Karl lost the stare-off, smirking and looking away.

Hiram is his handler. He has been for several months now. They got along easily, making formalities drop soon into the acquaintance.

"Shalom, Hiram."

The senior Mossad man set the phone on his lap. He twisted around and held himself there with an arm behind the passenger seat. In his fifties, Hiram is a former Israeli Defense Force (IDF) officer turned spy. He keeps a trim salt-and-pepper haircut, glasses, and a short beard. When he smiled at Karl, a toothy grin glistened behind a mustache that needed trimming as the hairs came down unevenly over his lip.

"Shalom, Karl. I've not seen anybody since I've been waiting. Shall we take a ride?"

"Yes, around the park and home for tea afterward."

Hiram chuckled. "As you say, sir." He faced forward, cranked the engine, feathered the clutch, and backed the car out.

Once they were on the road, he rolled his window up and pressed a concealed button under the dashboard. The Fiat's electronic countermeasures system energized. It masked their conversation from electronic surveillance. Most radio devices, such as bugs and trackers placed on the vehicle or their person, wouldn't function.

"We're screened, and I've got your assignment coming up," Hiram said without turning around.

The seat cushion next to Karl rose like a hatch, revealing a large compartment hidden underneath. Inside: a cell phone, passport, Bluetooth earbuds, wallet, and a tiny Ziploc baggy containing a microSD memory chip.

Who am I to be this time?

He scooped up the Samsung phone, replacing it with his deactivated iPhone.

Hiram glanced up at his mirror. "Your luggage is in the trunk. There's enough to last you one week, so be prepared to do some laundry during your stay. We're hoping this will take less than three weeks, but it depends on if the rabbit bolts or goes into hiding somewhere we don't know about."

He pushed in the clutch, and the car ground its gear a time or two before slipping into the next one with a clunk. "Damned gearbox. I'm keep meaning to have it looked at."

Karl turned on his new smartphone. While it booted, he picked out the passport and began flipping through it. His cover name is William Jones.

Not very original, but so common it'll render me invisible.

Next, he picked up and opened the wallet. There were five American twenty-dollar bills, a matching driver's license from South Carolina, and a Visa debit card. A piece of tape across it had the pin written in black Sharpie.

The car suddenly jolted hard. Startled, Karl fumbled the wallet as he grabbed the door handle and pressed his other hand flat to the seat.

"Dammit! Sorry, boss. Hopefully, whatever we hit didn't flatten my tire." Hiram squished his cheek against the window, futilely trying to inspect the tire.

"That scared the shit out of me," Karl said with a chuckle.

"Ah, I can't see a damn thing." Hiram jerked the wheel left and right a few times. "Feels okay. No flat. Sorry again. Go back to your thing."

Karl let the heat flash rippling through his body subside before resuming the inventory. The phone finished booting, displaying a home screen filled with standard icons for messaging, telephone, and various other apps. He flipped the phone on its side and found a microSD port, into which he slipped the supplied microSD card. It clicked into place. He turned the phone face up; its screen showed blank—another boot sequence to complete. Karl watched the city go by in the meantime.

After a minute or two, the phone vibrated. A rotating symbol of the Mossad appeared. Underneath the emblem, a graphical thumbprint. After touching the icon, it prompted him for his biometric input. He pressed a thumb to the phone's scanner. A basic white screen with black-lettered links listed in numerical order appeared. The title at the top read 'Operation: Palmetto.'

Link number one spelled 'Background.' Karl touched the link. The display changed, showing a long narrative describing this latest assignment. To his delight, the first thing it proclaimed was he'd be the lead agent.

He smiled to himself. This is something he'd waited patiently to achieve for two years since signing up for the Mossad. *I wish I could call Gabby and tell her I finally got an assignment as lead agent.*

"They must be shorthanded," Karl said wryly.

"Oh?" Hiram said, eyebrows lifting in the rearview mirror.

"Yeah, it looks like they've made me the lead agent, which means they must be desperate and/or shorthanded."

Hiram snorted. "Don't get your hopes up. It's no mistake. You've proven yourself quite worthy. You've got your stuff together far more than most of these young people they recruit. It was an easy recommendation when Tel Aviv asked me what I thought about you."

"Thank you. I appreciate the acknowledgment. It means a lot to me. I'd be lying if I said I wasn't a little anxious. Nervous, the more I think about it."

"You're welcome, and you'll do fine. It's just first-time jitters."

Karl fished in a pants pocket for his smokes, knocked one out, and pulled it free with his lips before resuming the mission brief on his phone.

Hiram drove them out of the city, into the countryside. Today's random route took them past a field of daffodils in full bloom. Each circuitous drive through and around Nuremberg with a new assignment provided fresh sights. The inconsistency of the rides helped throw off anyone following or trying to listen in on them. Hiram would return Karl to the airport when he finished sorting out the mission.

As he read, the assignment seemed straightforward. Doctor Vahan Nafisi is their target. An Iranian nuclear scientist. Tel Aviv said they received word he left Iran to attend a science convention in Nuremberg. Karl glanced at the date.

It looks like that happened the night before last.

Attempts to eliminate Nafisi failed in Iran. Now, Israel saw an opportunity to capture the man for interrogation. Karl is to depart Germany for the US immediately and link up with other agents assembling in Charleston.

I wonder who I'll have for a team? They would've taken in my scant experience and given me some junior people. Maybe one senior man. Or woman, as the case may be.

The dossier read:

"Vahan Nafisi, born in April 1958. Grew up in Tehran, Iran, with brother Hedyeh. Both married young, Vahan wedding his wife in 1976."

Gabby keeps dropping hints about wanting to marry. The scary thing is it isn't bothering me. We're so comfortable together. I could see us buying that house in the country. There's no way I'd do that without a marriage commitment. The problem is, I figured that would never happen.

"After he married, Vahan left his homeland to attend university in France for eight years, receiving a physics degree, then a doctorate in nuclear physics. Dr. Nafisi promptly returned to Iran, hoping he could put his new credentials to work profitably."

That would be terrible. Get married, then leave for eight years? I don't even know if I'm going to continue working for the Mossad if Gabby and I get married soon. Our relationship seems good so far. But I'm just getting started in this business.

"Not finding employment in Iran, Vahan and his family moved back to France, landing a nuclear power plant position. That job lasted five years until he got fired for getting into an argument with the boss and threatening to choke him. A visitor from the Iranian government came shortly afterward and made him a job offer."

"Jobless and disgruntled, he couldn't refuse the lucrative offer and returned to Iran. Things had changed. The revolution flushed out the entire previous regime. Now religious zealots ran the place, which suited him fine after his years immersed in Paris's debauchery. It felt like Allah's hand at work, guiding him home to a new world of purity and discovery."

How do they know that's how he felt? I wonder who had a conversation with him and jotted down his feelings for the record. Recorded phone conversations, maybe? Undercover agents talking to him?

"The brother, Hedyeh, left with his family when the revolution happened and went to America, where he now resides. Initial investigations turned up Hedyeh's home and business addresses. He is in the wholesale office equipment industry."

What the hell is the "wholesale office equipment industry?"

"Nafisi's wife and children were all killed when an Iraqi aerial attack destroyed the neighborhood they lived in, which left Vahan alone."

Unlit cigarette still hanging from his lip, Karl set the phone face up on his thigh and got a lighter out of his pocket. After cracking the window, he sat back and continued his study session. By the time he finished smoking the cigarette, he'd have completed reading over the mission background.

"Dr. Nafisi works for the Iranians at one of their nuclear weapons research facilities. He's in Nuremberg for a conference. The previous night, while a gala for the conference goers was in progress, facial recognition cameras at the airport picked up Nafisi. He got tailed, not detained. He surprised everybody by taking a flight to America."

I'm betting the man is making a run for it. And it's probably to his brother. They might be developing a spy ring. The conference was just a rouse to get him legitimately out of Iran and infiltrate Germany or America.

For Karl and the assembling team, it'd be a snatch-and-grab mission. If they find him. His travel itinerary had Charleston, South Carolina, as his final destination. Locate Nafisi, kidnap him, and spirit him out of the country. They're to be notified at the time what mode he'll travel out of the country. Most likely a submarine, according to the paperwork.

Submarine? How will we pull that one off?

Normally they'd dispose of the scientist, and the Israelis would have one less Iranian to worry about. Apparently, Karl's bosses had something else in mind for this specific scientist. When he finished the first cigarette, Karl lit another one.

The Samsung phone had typical apps, right down to a Facebook app with a phony profile and fake posts.

What's weird are the imaginary friends who reply to my counterfeit posts. Who are they?

He surmised they're likely computer-generated responses, as the app didn't connect to Facebook at all. Some of his fake friends' reactions were too human for comfort. All the apps on this phone were bogus. Even the EcoTaxi app.

Hiram glanced at Karl's reflection. "Okay, we're almost at the airport. Are there any questions I can answer?"

How did thirty minutes fly by like that?

"Know any good places to eat in Charleston?"

"I said questions I can answer. No, sorry, I've never been there myself. Your contacts there ought to know where to go. Maybe it's a husband-and-wife team. The wife might be a superb cook."

It'd be twenty hours of flying before Karl landed in Charleston. He glanced down at the dossier on his phone, next at his watch. "How long before we're back at the airport?"

"GPS says ten minutes."

Just enough time for another smoke.

Karl lit up another cigarette and watched the landscape roll past. It made his heartache knowing he'd be far from Gabby in a few hours. Older agents had warned him long ago about the dangers and pitfalls of getting attached to someone.

He'd been an accomplished player with a girlfriend in every port. This long-legged, sweet-faced German woman, who trusted him wholly, became a game-changer. She made him want to try for her. Made him want to be a better, faithful man to her. He'd even settled down with her in an apartment.

I may have lost my mind.

Hiram stopped the car at the airport departure curb, snapping Karl out of his reverie. "Here you are. Have a safe trip. See you in a few weeks?"

"Yes, hopefully, just a few weeks," Karl said as he crammed the laptop and other things into his leather backpack and popped open his door.

"Shalom!"

"Shalom," Karl said as he slid out of the car, leaving behind his real wallet and phone.

When he returned from this mission, they'd be waiting for him. For now, getting used to being Will Jones is the priority.

Karl mulled over his role as he strolled through the airport. The security lines were light. He reached the plane's gate with an hour to spare, using the time to immerse himself into the cover of Will Jones.

Some of his fake Facebook friends are support personnel, ready to assist him. Using the messaging app, he typed out a test message to Sherry, an in-house agent.

Will: Hi, I just wanted to say hello.

A few seconds later, his phone vibrated. He lifted it to see.

Sherry: Hello! Good to hear from you. I hear you're going on a trip ;)

Will: Indeed :(

Sherry: Aw, not your idea of a vacation?

Will: If it was plus one.

Sherry: LOL, you can decide if it's worth going back someday on holiday?

Will: We'll see. Talk to you later.

Sherry: Okay, safe travels.

Communications established, he turned his attention to the hotel app. He's staying at a gentrified old mill converted into a hotel. It had a rustic, old-time red brick motif to its exterior and interior.

You can just tell ghosts of some overworked mill workers must haunt the place.

It exuded a particular classic Southern charm Karl looked forward to checking out after settling.

Just another typical departure. I want this marathon plane ride to be over already.

An hour later, in his seat, he sat still for a moment or two. The rigmarole of getting to this point quieted down in his head. Tel Aviv had seen it fit to put him in the last row of the airplane, which meant he'll be one of the last people called to get on the plane.

One would think they'd want me on and off inconspicuously—Tomato, tomatoe. On first or last, it makes no difference. As long as no one knows who I really am. My cover is my first defense.

But keeping a low profile got taken to extremes in the Mossad. With good reason, of course, because of the dangerous nature of their job.

On the bright side, statistics indicate the back of the plane is safest.

He put his backpack under the seat in front of him, buckled his seatbelt, and slid the window shade up. Brilliant white sunlight made him squinch his eyes shut and push the blind back down. Sunrise had happened since his ride with Hiram. He donned his sunglasses hanging at the V of his T-shirt and slid the shade back up.

That's better.

Outside the plane, the ground crew loaded the last pieces of baggage. His black set of suitcases got tossed onto the luggage conveyor and disappeared from view—presumably into the plane's cargo hold.

Karl rubbed at the back of his neck.

Twenty hours to go. How could I have forgotten my neck pillow? One of those cheap little airplane pillows will have to do. Once the plane is in the air, I'll get one from the flight attendant.

For now, he watched out the window, and William Jones put his game face on straight.

III

Wednesday, April 10, 10:33 pm, Charleston, South Carolina

Karl, also known as Will Jones, finally arrived at Charleston International Airport after a 28-hour journey filled with boredom, discomfort, and connecting flights in Amsterdam and Detroit, Michigan. Even at night, the air is thick and humid with a faint ocean odor. His snug denim jeans felt like too much clothing. Upon arrival at the hotel room, he prioritized changing into shorts.

For now, he looked around as if he were seeking a sign directing him where to go. In reality, he examined as many faces as possible. If any of them turned up later, it could mean the difference between life and death by recognizing the familiarity and trip an alarm in his head.

He set his two black hard-shell suitcases down and dug his phone out of a pants pocket. After thumbing through its biometric security, he swiped to the EcoTaxi app and tapped the icon. His new leather Mossad-issued backpack straps still needed adjustment. He shrugged at its stiff straps while the app opened and displayed his current location on a small map. Underneath, a dialogue box asked him where he'd like to go. He tapped the screen; a recent history list popped up, pre-loaded with the traveling history of William Jones.

Standard cover story material.

The readout displayed his rideshare app history, providing details about his hotel, local attractions, and dining options. Tonight, he'd go to the hotel alone, like most first nights on assignment. No going out to eat. No visitors. No sightseeing. No phone calls. He'd study mission info, watch TV, and wait. That was about it.

That's fine with me. I just want to relax.

Each first night included a cooling-off period, in case other entities like the CIA or MI6 or whoever noticed his presence. The courtesy gave their allies a chance to say, "What the fuck?" Before they predicated the conversation with tasers and bullets.

I think it's a passive-aggressive form of begging for forgiveness rather than asking permission. Besides, it'd be embarrassing having another state agency break in as you're zipping up your ninja suit.

"To the hotel, it is," Will said to himself.

He selected the hotel cited in the mission brief. After confirmation, the app said it'd be thirty minutes before his ride arrived. With his driver on the way, he moved from the curb and posted himself in the smoking area. It comprised a plexiglass shack like a bus stop.

Two other nicotine addicts sat there already, smoking away and diddling on their phones, presumably waiting on a ride too. He'd been sitting for hours during the flight. The last thing he wanted to do was sit on some hard, crappy bench. He remained standing and lit up.

I wish I could let Gabby know I'm safe. I hate this detachment rule. Hiram will let her know. I just want to do it myself. Hear her voice. I never cared before like this. What's happened to me? What have you done to me, Gabriella?

The people, cars, and buses came and went for forty minutes before his phone buzzed with a notification that his ride would soon arrive. Will remained leaning against the smoke shack the entire time. He stood straight, grabbed up his suitcases, and moved to the curb.

A silver Hyundai sedan approached. He made eye contact with the driver, who waved. Will waved back.

When the car stopped, he saw "EcoTaxi" written in blue on a white rectangle. The letters and background were painted on the car, not a temporary magnet.

The driver's side passenger window opened, revealing a stern-faced man in his fifties with gray, bushy hair and a beard leaning towards the window. "William Jones?"

"Yes, sir. Are you Mr. Banks?"

"Yes, yes, that's me. Let's get your luggage in the back."

Will cut his eyes toward a *click* sound from behind the car. The trunk lid rose partway. Henry Banks popped up from the other side of the vehicle. His stern expression changed to the welcoming attitude of an American greeting a foreign tourist. "Mr. Will, welcome to America," he said with a flourish of his arms.

He went to the trunk and pulled the lid fully open. Will brought his luggage around. Henry grabbed the closest case, and together they slid them into the car and closed the lid.

He patted Will's shoulder. "Okay, let's get on the road."

Will smiled at him. "Let's go." He got in on the rear passenger side of the car.

Henry checked the navigation on his phone in a cradle attached to the windshield by a suction cup. Satisfied, he turned around. "How was your flight?"

"It was uneventful. Boring, really."

"Ah, well, you're here safe." Henry faced forward. "The ride will be about twenty minutes."

He put the car in drive, checked his mirrors, and stomped on the accelerator. When they were clear of the airport, Henry leaned forward, reaching under the dash with one hand to activate electronic countermeasures. He rubbed his hands together. "Okay, we're screened. Are you familiar with your cover?"

Will scowled. "What kind of amateur do you think you picked up just now?"

Henry flicked his eyes up to the mirror. "I don't know. Hence the reason I'm asking. No offense intended."

He's just doing his job and doesn't know me.

Will drew a breath. "Yes, I've familiarized myself with my cover. I'm Will Jones, a consultant that travels a lot between America and Europe."

Henry returned his gaze to the road. "Good. You wouldn't believe the dumb shits they send me sometimes. I feel like they're trying to blow my cover on purpose with those duffers."

Will chuckled and hoped this team would be a solid group of professionals. One never knew what one was getting until they were already there. At first, there would be a sense of disarray. But after a few days, everybody usually gelled. Or, at least, figured out everybody's limitations and compensated for them. Their Jewish heritage was often enough to keep even the most aggravating members on point. This time, Will would be the one in charge. All the responsibility rested on his shoulders.

God, I hope I'm ready for this level of responsibility. It's surreal planning to shanghai another human being, never mind going through with it. Killing him would be simpler, for sure.

"The rest of the team is still assembling. A couple of agents won't be here until tomorrow morning. I plan to pick them up when I pick you up."

Will gazed out the window. "It was a long flight. I'm happy to be on the ground. Even if it is in some humid hellhole."

"Hellhole? You'll like it here, Mr. Will. Charleston is a delightful town. Touristy, but a cool place to live. You get used to the heat and humidity."

Henry explained that he'd lived in the US for twenty years, integrating himself utterly into the American culture and scene. He moved around as needed. Like brief jaunts to neighboring regions to help with other operatives. He mostly assisted those doing the Mossad's riskier work when they were in the state of South Carolina.

"You're probably right. I'm just homesick already."

"Uh-oh, somebody has a girlfriend or boyfriend?"

Do I come off as gay?

Will scowled and smirked. "Yes, a girlfriend. She's made it difficult to leave these days."

"You should look into deep-cover fieldwork. You get to have a life while you're undercover. You also don't have to travel near as much."

"Yes, but you're gambling with your loved one's lives. Don't you think?"

A moment of silence passed between them. The statement was cruel, yet true. Both Will and Henry faced this reality - the loved ones of operatives were always at risk.

He tried to focus on the mission. Gabby occupied every other thought. From experience, he knew this "in-love" feeling waned over time. Part of him never wanted it to go away. He wished he could dial it back some.

Henry broke the silence. "Well, not so much here in America. Since you can own guns, you can protect yourself and your family. A few dozen security cameras and some friends close by help too. From what I read of the intel, our scientist just missed getting killed a while back in Iran. Somebody botched the takedown. Now they want him alive? And spirited out of the US? It sounds like somebody up the chain doesn't know what they want."

Will said, "Friends with guns always help. It's something to think about for the future. I couldn't imagine trying to attach a bomb to a moving car from a motorcycle. Whoever did it had balls of titanium. And they must be crazy. Kidnapping I can deal with." His stomach grumbled. Looking around outside the car, he said, "Can we stop somewhere for a bite?"

"Drive-thru only, my friend."

Later, while Will scarfed a chicken sandwich, Henry drove to the hotel, regaling him with his conspiracy theories, team members, and tentative schedule. He also grilled him on his cover. It made Will chafe.

Does he know I'm the lead? Maybe he thinks he's the lead? Perhaps I appear the newb I am? You'd think two years' worth of field experience got a little more respect.

Admittedly, he also found the lessons helpful in galvanizing his identity as Will Jones. By the time they reached the hotel, he'd crammed the wrappers from his meal back into the bag and gathered his things. Henry pulled in where the valet waited and put the car in park. He waved off the young black valet, who waved back and returned to the podium near the door.

Henry turned around to Will. "All right, here's the deal. Eventually, I will stop nagging you. Remember to lie low tonight. I'll return tomorrow to pick you up around ten. Go through the motions in the EcoTaxi app and all that malarkey."

Will glanced around before patting Henry's forearm. "Thank you. I'll see you in the morning. Shalom."

"Shalom."

He left the car, suitcases in hand, and headed towards the hotel's revolving door. He checked in and went straight to his room. Once inside, he dropped his bags by the door and sat on the bed.

Well, here I am. If people only knew how boring ninety-nine percent of clandestine work really is, they'd laugh at the next Bond movie.

He rubbed his face and tackled the next project, unpacking. If he used the place like it was his own apartment, it made it less foreign. He put his clothes away in the closet. Fifteen minutes later, he settled in with his laptop open and booting on the room's desk.

His computer had two personalities, like his phone. One is a civilian, the other a Mossad operative. With a biometric scan of his forefinger and memorized passkey, he entered Mossad mode.

Will occupied his evening with reviewing Dr. Nafisi's profile, satellite images of the brother's house, and pondering Gabby's whereabouts.

I'd guess she's sleeping right about now, as it's early in the morning back home.

He had the impulse to text her but chose not to act on it. He sighed. "Meine Liebe, how I wish you were here too." Will went back to the satellite images.

The man was supposed to die, but the institute had a change of heart. Lucky you, Mr. Nafisi. If you cooperate, I'd imagine you'll find freedom, eventually. Or at least I'd like to think so. They may drop you in the ocean in the end. What could you know that's so important that our own scientists can't figure out or already know? I suppose your knowledge of the Natanz facility could be useful intel.

Nafisi's brother's house was only a few kilometers from his business. His office was nestled in a compound filled with dozens of other non-retail businesses. He carefully examined the surroundings of both locations, considering various scenarios for breaking in, surveillance, and even attack and defense.

It's too bad we don't have any images from the ground. We'll have to put some cameras in place around the house. Or we could use the remote surveillance units. They might come in handy. I know the engineers at the institute always like feedback about one of their gizmos.

He picked up the phone and pecked out a note about cameras. As he thought about it, he added 'drone' to the list. Five minutes later, he had a list of seventeen items.

If he got four competent team members, he'd immediately order the camera placement and twenty-four-seven surveillance. The brother's workplace looked to be the best site to attempt a kidnapping.

With few witnesses and a secluded back door, it'd be relatively easy to pick him up. Assuming he ever went to his brother's office. We need a lot of surveillance data. Too many unknowns just yet to act.

Will leaned back in his chair and stretched. He bent an elbow down and checked his watch—11:18pm. With the time difference, the dregs of jet lag reared their ugly head.

I'm just going to lie down and try to sleep. A cup of tea might help.

The hotel provided a coffeemaker in his room with coffee and tea packets. Five minutes later, he had a steaming cup of tea. He sipped at it as he moved about the room, turning off lights, turning down the bed, and getting undressed. After all the lights were out, he checked outside his window. Being on the third floor, he's pretty safe from intrusion or easy observation. He peered up and down the street.

Nothing to see there.

Next, he listened at the door before cracking it open and peeking out.

All quiet here, too. It's time to get some sleep.

In bed under the covers, Karl spooned up to a pillow. He imagined it being Gabriella. Sleep took him in less than a minute.

IV

Thursday, April 11, 7:05 am

After a cup of coffee, Will kicked off his day with a four-kilometer run through the streets of Charleston early the next morning. He ran a square perimeter around the hotel a few blocks out. Along the way, he noted as much as possible, from coffee shops to pawn shops to the couple out for a morning run and the older woman walking her dog. He explored an assignment's surroundings when it was practical. It combined a sort of game with the mundane tasks of running for exercise and situational awareness.

The meters go by quicker that way.

He returned to the hotel, seemingly in no time, sweating profusely. He stopped at the hotel's buffet, loading some fruit, eggs, and yogurt onto a plate, then took it back to his room. After breakfast and a shower, two hours remained before Henry returned to pick him up.

The EcoTaxi app on his phone allowed scheduling a pickup. He set one up at 10:00 a.m.

All right, that leaves only one hour and fifty-five minutes to go.

Heaving a long sigh, he drummed his fingers for a few seconds, soon deciding to pass time scrolling through the mission brief.

They've got two drones and two robotic infiltration units for the mission, along with the five of them. Henry Banks and his wife will hang back as support, not getting too close to the action. Their position in the US had been a secret for two decades. Running around playing James Bond only got them exposed or, worse, killed. Their long-established residency helped legitimize their credentials.

He read over the team dossiers for a third time, starting with Arnold McGee. A five-year Mossad veteran with a background in surveillance and the assistant team lead. A good-looking man. More Arab-looking features than Jewish, he'd seen and done plenty in his time. This included data analysis, over-watch duty, and three instances in the commander's office because of undisclosed disciplinary issues.

Hence me outranking him, though he's been in longer. I wonder if there'll be friction? I also wonder just what he had done.

Next on the list is James Duvall. He looked vexed by too many sleepless nights and probably needed a lot of alone time. Duvall is a three-year veteran specializing in counterterrorism.

Nothing unusual in his file. These two already sound like decent operatives. We may be able to do this job quickly. By the end of the week, I could be back home with Gabby. Of course, I'm new to leading missions, so it's probably going to be a shitshow.

The last two agents, John Dickens and Kevin Abercrombie, are the computer and drone specialists. Both are young and inexperienced, with one year for John and six months for Kevin.

But the Institute only "chose the best."

Cynicism tainted Karl's outlook on people after gaining experience, despite being reasonably confident in their competence. His chief concern involved the naivety of new agents, something one wore off with the sandpaper of experience. It took years hardening a person to be ruthless.

I haven't even drawn my weapon in combat yet. God knows I've practiced enough.

In their quest to round up Nazi war criminals, the Mossad founder's legacy became legendary to clandestine operators around the globe. Those initial accomplishments set the bar intimidatingly high.

9:55 a.m. finally rolled around. Will put on his backpack, straps adjusted, and went down to the front entrance. He didn't wait long. At 10:01 a.m., Henry pulled into the hotel driveway at the wheel of a Dodge minivan. Music thumped inside the van as it lurched to a halt. Muffled laughter emanated from inside. "Henry, man, are the brakes new or something?"

The side door slid open, letting out a plume of smoke and the actual music volume. Arab pop tunes declared a jihad on Will's ears.

What? The? Fuck?

Three men inside broke into laughter, shouts, and catcalls. Henry bellowed something back from the driver's seat. The music drowned him out. When he reached for the volume knob, the man in the front seat swatted his hand away.

"Willlllll," they all said in unison. "Come, brother! Join our party!"

Hands beckoned, and Kevin Abercrombie slid over, giving Will the door seat. The men in the back seat were the rowdiest. The man up front twisted around. Will bent over and plopped into the van, dropping his pack on the floor.

"Drink?"

The voice came from behind. A half-empty bottle of vodka tapped on Will's shoulder. He scowled, leaning away and sliding the door closed. *They're drunk! They've got to be joking.* "No, thanks." He turned to the man next to him. "Kevin, good to meet you."

They shook hands while Kevin introduced the others. Pointing at each, he shouted their names over the music. "That's John Dickens upfront."

John offered his hand from the front. "Nice to meet you. Was your flight good?"

"It was long and boring but overall pretty painless," Will said as he shook John's hand.

"That's good; mine was the same. Got any news about the mission?"

Kevin said, "Yeah, has this guy we're after come here or not? Oh, and I think you know Henry. That's Arnold and James in the back. You can call him Jim, though. He says James sounds,"—he made air quotes —"too Britishy."

Will furrowed his brow. "Can we turn down the music?"

Henry dialed the volume down without getting swatted this time. "Sorry, your drunken mates had to have it loud."

"My drunken mates? Who is drunk?" Will said with a sneer.

He glanced at everyone in the van, his face filled with disbelief. When he turned to the men behind, they wore shit-eating grins. Jim let out a mouth full of cigar smoke. They both waved back at him innocently, in unison, Arnold making a futile effort at hiding the bottle of vodka between his legs. Will eyed them critically and shook his head before turning back to the front.

They aren't joking. Mossad officers should know better. And with some very junior agents around, too.

"I'd prefer everyone remain sober when on duty."

"Hey," Kevin said, raising his hands, "I'm totally sober, dude."

John said, "I'm dry too, boss. Those two are the only ones having fun. Can we stop somewhere and get some booze?"

Arnold scowled. "We're on duty?"

"Technically," John said, "we're always on duty when deployed on foreign soil. Henry, do you have anything besides beer to drink?"

Arnold and Jim commenced snickering. After a few seconds, Arnold cleared his throat. "Sorry, Mr. Will. William Jones, is it? Nice to meet you. We just got off a flight from Africa. We might've gotten bored and struck into drinking toward the end. There weren't even any good-looking stewardesses or whatever they call them these days. We're good, though. Right, Jimbo?"

"Yes, sir." Jim punctuated his reply with a beautiful, deep belch.

Arnold melted into an adolescent giggle until his face turned red.

Henry turned to John. "We're almost at my place. There's a liquor store down the street. After the meeting, we can make a run."

John sat back in his chair, folding his arms. "Sounds like a plan, my friend."

Will pinched the bridge of his nose and closed his eyes. "Dammit."

Henry saw his exasperation in the rearview. "Don't worry; I have plenty of coffee and homemade bread to get them right again. You see what I mean about the ilk they send me nowadays? A bunch of malingers!"

Arnold quieted them clumsily with his hands. "Guys, seriously, we're fine. We just had a few too ma —"

Henry made an abrupt turn, throwing Arnold into Jim. They resumed giggling. Jim pushed Arnold off himself.

"Did you see what just happened?" Arnold asked.

Jim nodded and faced the window, trying his best to get his composure as Will burned imaginary laser beams on their foreheads. His eyes darted back and forth between the two inebriated agents. They would've collapsed into salami slices if his eyes had indeed been lasers. Henry broke the tension by turning the music back up a little.

"Hey, everybody! Welcome to Charleston. Let's just get to my place, and everybody can have a beer. Sound good?"

Nobody responded. They rode together in relative silence for the brief trip to Henry's house. Will fumed. Arnold and Jim tried to sober up, likely hoping Will wouldn't be a prick for the rest of the mission. John and Kevin remained quiet, probably wondering what they had gotten themselves into as well.

Arnold said, "Hey, Will, we thought we had more time to sober up. Before we knew it, Hank was picking us up, and we were still rather lit. Are a lot lit. So then we were like, 'fuck it.' You know how it goes?"

"I... I hope this won't be what I can expect from you going forward."

He regretted the snotty comment as soon as the words fell out.

"Ha! You'll never know what to expect from me," Arnold said, pointing two fingers at his eyes, subsequently pointing them at Will.

Will took in a deep breath as Henry slowed the van. Arnold noticed an attractive girl walking along the sidewalk. He grabbed Jim's arm and halfheartedly tried to pull him over to the window. "Oh my god, would you look at that ass! I want her."

Ogling the woman too, Jim said, "Yep, she's not bad. Of course, you're a long way from even attempting the feat."

Together, they ogled her until they couldn't see the woman anymore.

"What? We're on Henry's street. Isn't that right, Henry? We're almost at your place, yeah?"

Henry glared at them in the rearview mirror. "Please, for the love of God, shut your mouth around her or anybody in this neighborhood, or I will tase you myself and ship you back to Israel in a swine crate! Are we clear, Arnold? Jimbo?"

A moment of silence hung in the air before everybody, even Will, sang, "Ooooooo!"

"We're on the shit list now," Jim said under his breath.

The crew erupted into laughter.

"I'm serious. Mine and my wife's safety depend on you thinking with the big-head instead of the little one."

Will cleared his throat. "Henry, I can guarantee we'll maintain your cover integrity. Isn't that right?" He glared back at Arnold and Jim. A stern countenance on his face told them he wasn't joking.

They both nodded profusely.

Arnold said, "My apologies, Henry. I'll behave myself and lust after her from afar."

Jim said, "I'll do the same and lust after her from afar too. Sir. Mr. Henry, sir."

Henry hissed. "Yeah, yeah, screw you, too. Just remember my warning." As he waggled a finger in the air, he brought the van to a near stop before turning into a narrow driveway leading to an old white three-story shotgun house.

Not much over six meters separated the homes. Styled differently, Henry's house had three stories rather than two, like his neighbors. The driveway squeezed between the houses leading to a concrete pad and garage around the back. Once the van was inside and the garage door back down, they would move int's home. They can do it unobserved through a covered passage leading from the garage to the house. An inconvenient addition; Henry's Mossad handlers insisted he build for privacy.

When the garage door slammed shut with a rattle, Will slid open the van's door and hopped out, scooping his backpack up as he did so. He slung it over one shoulder and stood ready to assist his comrades as if they were climbing out of a lunar lander.

First, Kevin emerged, then John and Henry. Henry had his phone out. He must close out each ride as if it were a legitimate rideshare. Finally, Arnold and Jim squeezed out from the back seat. There they all stood, forming a semicircle around the open van door.

Kevin, the nerd his is, said, "It's like the Fellowship of the Ring."

Arnold rolled his eyes. "Kevin, Kevin, son, you're not getting anywhere with the ladies talking like that."

Kevin smiled, his red face belying his embarrassment.

Will, not a self-proclaimed nerd, is also a fan of the Tolkien series. To show some camaraderie, he said, "One ring to rule them all."

Arnold groaned. "Christ, it's going to be a long mission."

Everybody laughed at that while Henry ushered them into the covered passage.

The tension bled off, replaced with jovial moods. The anticipation of a new mission had everybody excited. Even Will felt more at ease.

Jim broke into song. "Heigh-ho, heigh-ho it's off to spy, we go!" He sang as they marched through the passageway, single file.

Yvette, a middle-aged woman of slight build and deadly glare, barred their entrance with one arm behind her back when they reached the door. Henry patted her shoulder as he passed, and she removed the .357 revolver concealed behind.

"It's okay. They sound like idiots, but they're good kids," Henry said.

She held the door for everyone. She smiled at Will and said, "You had me worried for a minute there, Hank."

Yvette is one of the few people who can get away with calling Henry Hank.

"Its not often dwarves come to visit—especially such good-looking and loud ones. My, my, what a handsome bunch we've got this time. I usually shoot dwarves first and ask questions later." She sighed. "Losing my edge, I guess."

Will tried putting on an air of confidence. "Good morning, Yvette," he said with a smile, "I'm Ka—Will."

Yvette winked at him, holding the door open with a foot. Dressed in pink, knee-length shorts and a black T-shirt, she greeted everybody in turn. Kept handy in a cabinet next to the door, she stretched and slid her pistol back into its holster.

The interior of the house felt cold and dry compared to the outside. Decorated with knickknacks and various hand-painted pictures all around. A smorgasbord of folk art crap. The ubiquitous tinge of mildew hung in the air. The entire town, including his hotel and current location, smelled of mildew constantly.

Henry led them up the stairs, surrounded by handmade art and travel memorabilia, all the way to the roof. The roof door opened up onto a high walled patio. A white plastic umbrella table and chairs stood in the middle. LED tiki lights strung along the wall's top added a festive touch.

A person over 1.5 meters tall could see over the wall. Jim, shorter than the rest, stood on his toes to take in the panorama. They had a wide view of the city in all directions. They could begin planning with everyone in attendance. Henry waited until everyone got seated.

"This area is a safe zone for us to talk and plan. Short of a drone flying right up to the wall, no one can observe us nor hear us thanks to the walls and embedded electronic countermeasures within the lights lining the wall's top edge. We have a satellite connection disguised as that solar panel." He pointed to a dark rectangular panel protruding from the other end of the patio.

"And various radio transmitters are at our disposal. All properly licensed under the US Federal Communications Commission codes."

Henry prattled on for ten minutes, describing the spook features of the house. When he noticed Kevin nodding off, he held up a printed message and waggled it. "This, my friends, is the message from on high. No drum rolls, please. It'll answer the question: Has this Iranian pig come running, or did a lot of money get wasted on plane tickets by the Mossad?"

He paused, kept the sheet of paper between two fingers, and put on reading glasses hanging from his neck. After scanning the note and clearing his throat, he looked out over the audience, focused on him.

Kevin threw his hands up. "Aw, come on! Quit teasing us already."

V

Henry, referring to the note, said, "According to the institute, Nafisi boarded a plane bound for Detroit on Tuesday at 6:00 a.m. That would match chronologically, putting him here in Charleston that night. Assuming that's his intention."

Will's heart sank a little. *Damn. No chance of getting back home early now.*

After Henry read the message aloud, they passed it around until it came back to him. Their course set, he put it into an empty coffee can on the table. Scorch marks inside the cylinder spoke of previous missives destroyed the same way.

Henry, pulling a lighter from his pants pocket, picked the can up and tilted it to ignite a protruding corner. With a few seconds flame applied, the paper caught fire. Satisfied it burned intensely enough, he set the can on the table and dug in his pocket again. He pulled out his smartphone this time. "We've got some housekeeping to do first."

He pecked and swiped at his phone for a moment. Yvette and Henry had a small refrigerator on the patio in a corner. While Henry was busy on his phone, she offered drinks and stayed by the swing. Will felt impressed that Arnold and Jim were keeping quiet. They had the haggard look of people on the downslope of inebriation.

The private rooftop's acoustics made it easy to hear a discussion around the table. Before sitting down, she stepped forward, holding up a bottle of iced tea over the tabletop. "Cheers, everybody. We're glad you all made it here safe and sound. Thanks be to God."

"Here, here," Arnold said, leaning forward to clink Yvette's bottle.

The others around the table made similar toasts and cheers, tapping her tea with sports drinks, a Diet Coke, and a plastic bottle of water.

"And just so you know, the rest of your drinks and food will be self-serve unless I tell you otherwise," she said. "This isn't your mom's, and I'm not your mom, so clean up after yourselves like grown-ups. The same goes for the bathrooms. If you mess it up, you better clean it up, or I'll come looking for you. And you won't like it, mind you." She held up a hand, ticking off points with her fingers. "No parties, no girls, no smoking—any kind of smoking. You smokers never clean up after yourselves, and I end up picking up your damned butts."

Jim raised a hand. "What do you mean, no girls?"

"I mean, you have hotels. Don't bring anyone here. Ever. No friends, etcetera. If you must smoke, do it before you come here. I've tried to be nice about it in the past, but I always end up picking up the mess. And answering the front door to girls you've met that are looking for 'this guy who, like, lives here.'"

Will heaved a sigh. "Okay, we get it. Everybody cleans up their mess. And no girls or boys. I want to--"

"I'm not finished," she said, with a glare at Will. "If you wouldn't mind keeping quiet a few minutes more, I will continue." He stared back, mouth agape. She looked away to the others, resuming her diatribe. "You'll arrive and leave together in the van or another approved vehicle marked with the EcoTaxi logo. None of you are to be seen here at any time. Furthermore, make sure to be armed at all times, with at least a blade of sufficient length to be lethal.

"My hands are deadly weapons," Arnold said, gesturing karate chops.

Yvette's withering stare shut him up, too. "Be armed, at all times," she reiterated, "and one last thing: I go to bed at ten every night. Our bedroom is underneath this patio. Unless we are actively overseeing an operation, all get-togethers will come to a close at 9:30 p.m. Sharp. Or--"

"--we'll have to deal with you," Arnold said, picking up where he cut her off.

Henry stood and faced his wife. "Thank you, Yvette. I'll take it from here."

She gave him a nod, returning to her perch on the glider swing, tucking one foot under a butt cheek as she landed on the cushions.

Henry turned back to the others. "You'll understand our insistence that you be very careful and considerate of our situation. Anything that draws too much attention could force us to shut down or threaten our lives. "So, tomorrow morning, there will be a security briefing in the kitchen. We'll tour the house and explain more details as we go." Looking over the rim of his glasses, he directed a flat hand at Will. "And this man is your fearless leader. They're all yours, Mr. Will."

The others gave a good-humored golf clap.

Yvette's rudeness had wrangled Will. *I'll have to watch myself and respect their concerns. But what of the others? Will they look out for Henry and Yvette? No matter what, why are they THIS paranoid? Too much time undercover? How do you not lose your whole self and identity?*

When he snapped out of his thought thread, he found himself already on his feet. "Thank you, Henry." He lifted a plastic bottle of Diet Coke to the surrounding agents with a smile. "Thank you all for your service to Israel. It's an honor being here together as God's chosen people." He lowered his drink and sat, scooching up close to the table, resting his elbows. "Let's get down to business, shall we? The first thing on my list is surveillance. We need to get eyes on the brother's house and place of business."

Jim said, "Wow, no intros? Aren't we going to stand up and say our names? What in the hell is an office equipment wholesaler, anyway?"

The team received the same encrypted mission brief on a microSD chip like Will. He snapped his fingers and pointed at Jim. "I was wondering the same thing."

Furrowing his brow, Jim asked, "You actually want to do intros?"

Chuckling, Will said, "No. I was referring to the office equipment wholesaler." He picked up his phone and read the screen. "It's likely a cover if I had to put money on it."

Arnold said, "Apparently, the brother, Hedyeh Nafisi, buys and sells wholesale used fax, printers, and copy machines. Like auctions or leasing companies. I think he repairs them and ships them overseas. Either to Iran or South American countries." Arnold shrugged and glanced at Will, who smiled, encouraged by one agent gaining intel on their own initiative.

"Yes, that's all correct. I did some research and found an eBay site owned by Hedyeh. That's where he sells the machines. From what I can tell, given the volume of sales he has, Hedyeh is operating a thriving business."

He unlocked his phone and brought up some notes with forty-two pages of information he'd gleaned from the Internet earlier. Everything from the post office Hedyeh used to what gas company serviced his house and office.

A local mosque website had a group photo. The caption listed the brother as one of those in it. He also shared information from credit checks. Hedyeh had several credit cards and bank accounts. Will turned his phone around to show a credit check app's results.

"No significant debts other than the office and his house. A background check came up negative too. He seems to be legitimately living the American dream. Self-employed and owning a home. He's paid his bills and obeyed the law. Except for a couple of traffic tickets, all for speeding." Will shrugged. "He's as normal as they come. I don't think we've got anything other than a normal guy. That could mean they're well trained. We'll keep watch on him and, if at all possible, keep him ignorant of his brother's fate when we grab him."

Kevin said, "What a perfect cover. Everything's so squeaky clean that it looks suspicious."

Arnold said, "Well, somebody's been doing their homework. How'd you come up with all that already?"

"As we all should have," Will said, making a point of looking at each team member. In his mind, it went without saying—a leader should do his research. Yet he researched for every mission, even when he was the lowliest agent onboard. Those previous roles had been passive and involved in little clandestine activity.

What caliber of agents are these people if they don't do the basics automatically? If you will not do the job well, why bother? I'm not being too hard on them, am I? We're all pros. At least, I think we are.

"I've been studying, too," Arnold said, face pouting. "I knew about the fax machines."

"Damn, what would we do without you, Arnie?" John said.

"You'd damn well get killed."

"Everybody, please, it's all-important to pay attention to the details," Will said. "We might pull this off with no hitches and look like heroes. I've got a rough plan figured out. Take notes or pay close attention. We'll split up into two teams. One will recon the office while the other prepares the equipment."

Arnold said, "We could go in as pest control, plant bugs, and get out."

Will rubbed at his chin. "That would require too much exposure. I want to save the pest control cover for more overt operations. We have two drones and their deployable hardware at our disposal."

"Those things are tricky to use," Arnold said. "Just do it the old-fashioned way and keep it simple. Works practically every time."

"Yes," Will said, "like in Salt Lake City last year? High-altitude stealth surveillance would've kept those agents out of the Americans' hands. Now they're detained in undisclosed locations. They were installing listening devices at a target's apartment and got caught by a robot home assistant called Albert or something."

"Alexa," Yvette said, correcting him.

"Yes, an Alexa unit alerted the target, and the police showed up to find a Mossad agent in the middle of searching the place."

Arnold, scoffing, said, "Yeah, yeah, I know, but those guys were unlucky amateurs. I've got this down."

Will shook his head. "We'll only insert automated units. There will be no breaking and entering. The less we touch, the better."

"What if the law finds those mobile things the drones deploy?" Arnold asked, hands raised.

"They're made with off-the-shelf parts. It's unlikely to be traced directly back to anybody," Will said, folding his arms.

Arnold put his hands up in surrender; his face told Will he didn't enjoy having his ideas dismissed. He's a clever, good-looking, extroverted man. Many would be content to let him lead and shoulder all responsibility. Every now and then, Arnold clashed with someone like Will Jones. The kind of agent who is smart and in charge, instead of him.

Will could tell he'd dented Arnold's ego. *Because he assumed he'd run roughshod over my command, I'm expected to care?* "Arnold, I respect your opinion; however, on this point, I'm firm. Remote surveillance only."

Will turned to Henry, eyebrows raised. "Are the drones and deployable units available for inspection?"

Henry nodded and stood. "Yes, sir, they're in here."

He shuffled past the seated agents to a plastic storage cabinet. Its texture looked wooden. It didn't come across as big enough to hold much more than a broom or two. Henry stooped into the closet and removed a false backing. John was closest to him.

Holding the back panel out to John, Henry said, "Here, stand this over there." He ducked, disappearing inside the cabinet. A moment later, he backed out, dragging a rectangular, black, plastic two hundred by fifty centimeters carrying case.

Kevin said, "Wow, it must be a lot bigger on the inside."

James and Arnold scooted their seats apart, giving Henry some room. He stopped dragging the case and spun it a quarter turn. Inside, disassembled and packed in foam peanuts—a dirigible drone. It had an empty tri-chambered helium gas bag encased in a black skin with turbofan motors to attach, carbon fiber framework, and cables.

John clucked his tongue. "We're gonna be up all night, putting that together."

Henry said, "Indeed, and there are no instructions."

Kevin said, "What? It's supposed to come with them."

Arnold laughed cynically. "Yes, I rest my case."

Will patted the air with his hands. "Everybody relax. We've got all the time we need. It's been a while, but I've put these together before, and it's not that difficult. Once you know what to do." He turned back to Henry. "How about the deployable units?"

Henry held up a finger as he disappeared into the closet like a grown-up trying to fit into his kid's playhouse. He reemerged, dragging another black plastic case. John and Kevin closed the dirigible box and hefted it together, moving it clear.

Henry positioned the second case where the other had been and opened it similarly. Inside, wrapped in translucent plastic bags, the two deployable units rested in foam cradles.

Henry reached in and lifted one out. "It is light as a feather. I didn't expect that. I think the box is heavier than these two things combined."

Will held out his hands to receive the deployable mobile unit. He glimpsed a four-legged, fur-covered animal silhouetted inside the bag and set the thing on the plastic table. After making sure it'd stand, Will gripped the plastic, ripping it open like a bag of Doritos. With the plastic torn, he stood staring down into the bag. The others leaned in for a gander.

Arnold laughed loudly. "What the ever-loving hell is that supposed to be?"

<u>VI</u>

"It looks like the Velveteen Rabbit," Jim said.

"More like Bill the Cat," Arnold said.

"It's state-of-the-art robotics that will enable us to get close to the target without alerting them or the neighbors," Will said.

Arnold and Jim had a hearty laugh at that one. John and Kevin finished getting the cat out of its bag and stood it on the table. Up close, its gray tabby coat obviously not cat fur. Will reached for it. It felt rough, like a bath sponge, as he squeezed and poked at it. The whiskers kinked, and ears not in sync—the cat looked terrible.

"You've got to be shitting me. This... this thing is going to do surveillance?" Arnold asked.

The incredulous tone and sneer on his face made Will heave a sigh. *His incessant criticism is getting old.*

John and Kevin started talking simultaneously. Kevin deferred to his senior. John said, "These cats were amazing at the Negev training center. You will not believe what they can do until you see it."

Arnold rolled his eyes and shook his head. "I've had plenty of shit sandwiches served up to me, too. And I bit into them like an idiot. The tech stuff is unreliable at worst and lucky at best. Keep it simple. Tried and true. Then they hand us this. What the hell is this called?"

Kevin perked up, turned toward Arnold, and said, "Since it isn't exactly manufactured, it doesn't have an official designation. We just called them cats: cat one and cat two, etcetera. Anyway, the tiny computers I'm going to install are where the institute really invested. It makes them glorified smartphones with legs. You'll see it in an hour or so. Once I get one of them online and update it's firmware."

Jim scratched his head and looked down at the cat without comment.

John said, "I'll get started on the drones. Will or Arnold, would one of you help me layout the frame?"

Will said, "Yeah, I'll help you."

Arnold lifted the other cat from the container and held it up, giving it a critical once over. "You won't need any help, will you, Kevin?"

"Nah, it's a one-person job, especially if you haven't had any training. We're definitely going to need more room in the van. Can you remove the seats or something?"

Arnold glared like he wanted to smack him for having the nerve to order him around. His eyes flicked around the group, some watching their exchange while others did not. His eyes met Will's.

Will didn't break the stare as he spoke. "Arnold, why don't you help John layout that frame? Also, I want you to take the drone team to a place outside the city to familiarize ourselves with their functions. The property has lots of open space for flying and driving these things. It's not far." Will broke off the stare, turning to Henry. "You know the way, so you'll have to go with them."

"Yep, I'll drive them out. We can shoot guns while we're there, too. The property is enormous. There's nothing much there except a small old house."

"Sounds good. Let's look at the van. You guys work on figuring out these drones. We'll get the van ready."

With that, Will stood and surveyed the busy crew before going downstairs with Henry in tow. In short order, they had the back seats out of the minivan. It had ample room for four people, two robot cats, five computers, and two shipping containers with drone equipment. Henry concluded they needed an additional truck for the blimp drone due to lack of space.

An hour later, they emerged onto the rooftop patio. Kevin turned excitedly to Will and waved him over. "Perfect timing, boss. The first one is rebooting now.

It'll come up in 'cat mode.' That's where it acts like a cat independently. Sort of like a screen saver for autonomous robots."

"We'll have control, correct?" Will asked.

"Oh, yeah, yeah, but when you're not driving it, it'll act like a cat."

Arnold said, "I don't know about the cats, but I like the drones. Mini-dirigibles, they are! They'll be quiet as church mice. It's given me some ideas about what we can do with them."

Will nodded approvingly, everyone pitching in and getting things together. He stopped at the head of the table, hands in pockets, waiting for the cat to reboot. *This group of strangers may still have hope. I'd expect no less from institute graduates. Lack of supervision in the field leads to unraveling agent behavior.*

The cat moved and drew his attention along with everybody else. Something about its articulation struck everyone as eerie.

"Here it comes," Kevin said. "Check this out, guys."

Arnold, John, Jim, and Henry all dropped what they were doing to come and watch. Yvette had gone off to watch one of her shows, missing the demo. The cat twitched, straightened, and oriented itself; Head leveling and looking more natural. The front paws evened themselves and came together in front. As it squatted on its haunches and looked around, the tail flicked in typical cat fashion—gradually undulating with a mind of its own. It looked at each one of them. Kevin checked the telemetry feeds and found their six pictures in a facial recognition database.

"The fucking cat just scanned us all, didn't it?" Arnold said.

"It sure did," Jim said. "Kevin, you got..."

"Yep, it got us all. Here, let's see patrol mode. I'll set it to go around the patio. Just gotta click here, and that should do it."

They watched with anticipation. The cat obliged by sitting back and licking its balls. As best a ball-less robot cat could do.

Arnold lost it. "Aaaaaah, I love it! Holy shit! That's fucking hilarious!"

All of them laughed. Eventually, the cat stood up on all fours, hopped off the table, strolled to the glider swing, and jumped onto it. The humans stood, mouths agape.

Arnold said, "This is some next-level tech. Where are the goggles?"

Kevin said, "Uh, I haven't tr--"

The cat laid on the swing, curling like a real one on a cushion.

Arnold said, "Now, if it purrs—"

"Actually," Kevin said with a finger raised, "it can play cat sounds. Which includes purring." Kevin reached for his laptop.

Arnold stopped him. "That's okay, son. Let it be. I want to see it move around more. How fast is it?"

"They're as fast as an actual cat," John said. "Not quite as agile, but pretty damn good. Kevin, have it run over to the other end of the patio under the table."

Kevin's fingers hammered away on a laptop's keyboard. After a few moments, he stopped, his eyes scanning over data scrolling up the screen. A map window appeared; he reached up and touched the screen, which showed a rendered version of the patio, and set waypoints.

The cat stirred, uncurling itself. After scanning the patio, it leaped off the swing. It shot through their chair legs, under the table, and out the other side. A meter from the wall, the faux feline leaped, plastic paws clacking against the wall, bouncing off to make a clumsy landing on all fours. Once it got its footing, it stood still, head scanning, tail waving.

Jim began clapping and laughing. "That is awesome. How long will a charge last? Can it run far?"

John said, "It can last two hours between charges if it's using a lot of energy. If it's just sitting and watching, it can last days."

"That has got to be the coolest thing I've seen in a long time," Will said.

Arnold snorted. "I'll have to admit that it's pretty damned neat. It's tech, nonetheless. It's as liable to fail at critical moments as work."

He stepped over to the cat, squatting next to it as if he were going to pet a tame animal. The cat looked up at him, cocking its head in curious-animal fashion. Arnold snorted and reached out to pet it. Its eyes closed in contentment; he pulled his hand back and stood. "Fuck me; they are creepy. You'll take some getting used to, you zombie cat."

Will rubbed at his chin and turned to Kevin. "Have it come right here to this spot on the table? They're supposed to maneuver around obstacles autonomously."

Will pointed in front of himself, near a burn mark on the plastic table's surface.

"No problem," Kevin said.

He touched his screen once, and a second later, the cat began walking forward. Upon reaching the table's edge, it jumped onto the tabletop. It sauntered to the exact point Will indicated, sat down, and began licking a front paw. Without a tongue, it only moved its head and lifted its paw.

Arnold said, "Boys, we need to get this gear packed up and into the van. How long do you think it'll take loading everything up? I take it the van is ready?"

"Yes, we took out all but the front seats. The van is wide open. It'll still be cramped."

"Don't we have another vehicle to use?"

Henry said, "Yes. The blimps are going in the truck. We prefer to limit vehicle traffic to maintain the location's remoteness and obscurity. So, just those vehicles it is. It's not a long drive. Besides, there will only be four of us."

Jim looked at Will. "What are the two of us going to do?"

"We're going to check out both locations in person this once. A single instance shouldn't cause any alarms. We'll need a car." He turned to Henry, eyebrows raised.

"You can take the Hyundai. The one I picked you up in at the airport."

"That'll be perfect. Let's pack everything together and leave separately. Jim and I will leave first."

Arnold moved to a shipping container and flipped open the top. "All right, gents. Let's get to it."

VII

Thursday, April 11, 1 pm

Will and Jim bade the others good luck after loading the van and left in the Hyundai. The tinted windows weren't so dark the car's interior wasn't visible during the day. It was enough that Jim scrunched down in the front seat, hiding until they got out of Henry's neighborhood.

No one would recognize him here in Charleston, but at Henry's directive, they were to at least try to stay hidden. The EcoTaxi logo on the front doors covered by blank, color-matched magnetic placards. It looked ubiquitous around Charleston, especially among rideshare entrepreneurs.

"Okay, Jim. We're clear."

Jim uncurled some and lifted his head high enough to peek out the car window. Seeing all was safe, he sat up straight and put his seatbelt on. Will lit a cigarette, rolled down the window, and hung his elbow on the sill. Warm, humid air tinged with tobacco smoke whipped around them.

"Where are we going first?" Jim asked.

"Let's do a flyby of the business. We'll take a few pictures and look for landing zones and obstructions for the drone."

"And then, the house?"

"Yes, we'll recon the house afterward."

Using an app on his phone, Jim navigated. He held it out in his left hand for Will to follow. Ten minutes later, they turned into the complex.

"It says we follow this street back through a couple of curves; then, the office will be on the left."

An access road meandered through a cluster of one-story, multi-office units. Each building, constructed of red brick with glass frontages, had a letter designation. Two rows of parking spaces paralleled the road in front of the offices.

They did a flyby of Hedyeh Nafisi's building. Several businesses occupied this unit lettered D. A driveway provided access to the parking lot. Nafisi's company lay at the end: D-6.

Jim squinted at the glass front door with its tiny white vinyl decals spelling out Nafisi Wholesale. An amateur had applied them, as they weren't straight and even. Jim snapped pictures with his phone as they passed. The road soon ended in a cul-de-sac.

Will turned them around in the cul-de-sac, flicking his cigarette out the window. This time, they dared pulling into the parking lot that served building D. Since it's a public workplace, their presence and even repeated passes shouldn't draw the slightest bit of attention. Although they'd prefer not to be seen by the Nafisi's.

No cars parked in front of D-6. Will pulled into a space. Jim got out and scoped the front door lock, returning quickly. As he slid back into the car, he said, "Regular lock. Shouldn't present any picking problems."

Next, they drove around back via an alleyway between C and D used by delivery trucks. The backside comprised a wide-open concrete lot, big enough for semi-trucks to turn around and back up to the loading docks. Another set of buildings mirrored this one's style on the opposite side of the lot.

Nafisi Wholesale's rear comprised a roll-up garage door and an adjacent door with D-6 stenciled in black letters. This unit, along with a few others, didn't have a loading dock. They stopped at the curb, demarcating the rear lot. In front of them, grass, palmetto bushes, and pine trees filled their field of view with D-6 to their right.

Jim, taking in the area, asked, "What do you think?"

"I think I know why they called it 'operation palmetto.' They're everywhere. This place is perfect if we're so lucky to nab him here. Nafisi may never come to this place. Who knows? I hope they come here. Preferably at night."

"I've got pics. There's tons of foliage to take cover. A night-grab will be straightforward and easy." He twisted around, scanning the building until his head went out the window. "I don't see many cameras. Just some that look at specific doors. And Nafisi is too cheap to bother with a camera. How convenient." He looked at Will and smiled.

Will scratched at his cheek a moment. "Yes, very convenient. I'd bet money the cheap bastard isn't even paying for an alarm service. Let's move on to the house."

They left the office park and made the six-kilometer drive to the Nafisi residence. The flat landscape, with tall, skinny pine trees growing like weeds dominating the scene. A thick layer of palmetto bushes with spikey light-green palm fronds covered the ground beneath the pines.

The homes in the neighborhood weren't new. All of them were squat, single-story, three-bedroom, two-bath family homes. It wasn't seedy or dangerous. It's a place where ordinary people live: ordinary people and some particular Iranians.

It gave Will a pang of guilt, knowing that they're about to disrupt the Nafisi's lives by kidnapping one of them. However, Iran is a vociferous enemy that would like nothing more than to witness every Jew's death. Will had been to Iran once. He found it to be one of the most nerve-racking and scary places to operate.

Ever since the Stuxnet virus, back in '09, Iran locked down hard on espionage. With the Americans' help, Israel infected Iranian computer networks with a malicious virus later coined Stuxnet. It destroyed millions of dollars' worth of centrifuge equipment.

Several Mossad agents got swept up in security dragnets afterward. Not that Karl blamed the Iranians. Some claimed Stuxnet set back the Iranian nuclear program by three to five years. Will shook himself and focused back on the task at hand.

Jim, counting the house addresses, slapped Will on the arm. "There it is. On the left." He nodded at a yellow stucco house with an attached carport. A gold, early 2000s VW Jetta sat under it.

Will slowed as they passed, allowing Jim to get pictures. A door to the carport suddenly opened.

They accelerated down the street, then slowed after passing a few places. The Jetta backed out in the rearview mirror. Jim twisted around to watch the car pull away.

"It's the brother, Hedyeh. I'm sure of it." The grin on Jim's face told Will they're thinking the same thing: follow the brother.

He pulled into the next driveway, backed out, punched the gas, and received a chirp from the front tires as they surged forward. When they caught sight of Hedyeh's car again, Will slowed and let him go through a stop sign before stopping extra long at the same sign ten seconds later. Both men kept their eyes glued to the Jetta.

This is a lucky break. I hope he's not just going out for milk and bread.

Will got his cigarettes out and lit one. Hedyeh stopped his Jetta at the next intersection and made a right turn. When they couldn't spy him anymore, Will floored the accelerator to catch up. He brought the car to a screeching halt at the same intersection a few seconds later.

"Okay, I see him. He's still on this road," Jim said, pointing in the direction Hedyeh had gone.

Will pulled out onto the road and followed. They had about half a kilometer between them and settled into tailing the VW. Hedyeh took them out of the area, onto the Savannah Highway, which brought them to the Ravenel Bridge. As soon as they were over the bridge, he exited, following signs to Patriots Point.

Before long, they approached an entry gate to the USS Yorktown on permanent display here. Their quarry paid and pulled through. He'd driven a hundred meters ahead when they stopped at the entrance and paid their parking fee. Will crept toward the parking lot to keep their distance.

"Why do you suppose he came here, of all places?" Jim asked.

"I was wondering the same thing. All I can think of is security in a public place. It'd be difficult to bring a weapon here. Hey, there's a case in the back seat. It's got a pair of smart glasses in it. Get them out for me. I'm going to follow him. You hang back in case he leaves without me knowing."

Without a word, Jim retrieved the glasses as asked. Hedyeh parked close up to the visitor center. Will parked several rows over and much further out. By the time he threw the car into park, Jim had his glasses ready and handed them over. He donned and synced them with his phone. A gold ring had a touchpad for moving a cursor in augmented reality and clicking on things like a camera button. The control ring had a large diameter, fitting loosely on his right middle finger. Tiny Bluetooth earbuds went into each ear. All connected, he dialed up Jim's phone.

Jim answered and brought the phone to his ear. "City morgue, you kill 'em, we chill 'em."

Will snorted a small laugh. "I read you loud and clear, too." He exited the car, heading for the visitor center—his smart glasses darkening automatically in the bright sunlight.

"Jim, I see there are some tables and a snack bar. Move to that position. I think you'll be able to see the comings and goings much better."

He heard some rustling sounds before Jim's voice came through his earbuds. "Yeah, okay. Moving to the tables."

When Will got up to the visitor center, he glimpsed Hedyeh. *Grumpy-looking and bald, with a thin gray mustache.*

Nafisi bought a ticket and walked through the security gate, passing on the souvenir picture they tried to force everyone to take.

Will turned and approached the woman at the ticket window. "One adult for the Yorktown." She taped a wristband on him to wear during the self-guided tour.

He hustled through security. By the time Will strolled along the causeway leading to the Yorktown, Hedyeh had reached the other end. He passed from view, climbing the stairs. Will slowed his walk, taking some pictures of the enormous ship.

He caught another glimpse of Hedyeh before he disappeared onto the giant airplane elevator at the top. During its years of service, countless aircraft raised and lowered on that elevator. These days, it served as an entrance to the floating museum—a door within the hangar door led inside.

Two steps at a time, Will bounded up the stairs. He slowed at the landing, making sure Hedyeh wasn't standing inside the hangar bay door. Seeing the coast clear, Will proceeded inside.

Dozens of vintage warplanes from World War II to Desert Storm filled the hangar along with displays of various heroes and events.

I can't believe the enormous structure can float, let alone sail the seven seas.

"He's still alone. I'm continuing inside."

"Roger that. Nothing exciting here. I've got a burger and fries. Oh, and there's a school group that looks suspicious. Should I take them out?"

Will stopped in his tracks. His cellular signal diminished significantly inside the metal ship. "What?"

"Ha! Nothing, boss. I was kidding. Nothing is going on out here."

Hedyeh moved toward the aft end of the ship's hangar. His attention was on the history and displays, with his back to Will. When he checked his watch for the twentieth time, Will felt sure he intended to meet someone.

The man made a beeline from home. Why would he do that other than to meet someone? There's the off chance he's a US Navy buff. Not likely. Hedyeh has a reason for being here other than nostalgia.

Will followed him through the ship's hanger for half an hour, filtering through the tourists, who provided excellent cover. When he had opportunities, he photographed Hedyeh using his ring and glasses.

They're all snapshots of the solitary man. Nobody has approached him yet. He hasn't even so much as answered a phone call.

Finally, Hedyeh glanced around before stepping through an open watertight door. Will moved toward the door, counting to thirty. He stepped over its bottom edge with as much casual indifference as possible. If Hedyeh waited on the other side, Karl could bluff his way through. Fortunately, the man didn't stop inside. He had climbed some steep steps up to another level, following signs directing tourists to the flight deck.

Will listened for any movement above. Only the diminishing sounds of Hedyeh's footsteps. He climbed the stairs and found himself in a cramped compartment with another set of stairs leading up. A passageway led elsewhere in both directions. To prevent tourists from getting lost, chains hung across many doorways. When he looked through the cordoned-off openings, he spotted a few people in parallel passages across from him.

Upon reaching the stairwell's flight deck level, he surprised two men loitering near the door that led outside. Spinning around to glare at him, they said nothing.

Could they be watching Nafisi, too? They're certainly acting suspiciously.

He smiled, nodded, and continued to climb up to the bridge.

There's a chance they aren't Americans between their glare, beards, dark eyes, and olive complexions. Those two didn't seem like the type to come here. They could've been checking out a girl's ass for all I know. I'll remember their faces for future reference, though.

An icon in his glasses flashed, showing no signal. Will frowned as he heard the connection with Jim drop. He sought a vantage point on the vacant bridge to observe Nafisi. The glaring sun caused his glasses to go dark again. When he found Hedyeh, all he could discern were his feet and lower legs from under a helicopter parked toward the ship's aft. Another pair of feet and legs stood in front of Hedyeh.

Who's this? Looks like another man?

Through the helicopter's cockpit windows, he caught sight of their embrace.

That has to be Vahan Nafisi! If only they'd come out from behind that helicopter for a positive ID.

"Jim, I think..."

The stairs rattled loudly.

Someone is coming. Will pretended to enjoy the view, barely able to keep his eyes off the brothers. One man he'd seen earlier emerged from the stairwell. The man stared straight at him, his face expressionless as he followed Will's gaze. They moved away from the helicopter. He lost sight of them altogether and leaned toward the windows.

"You seem inordinately interested in someone," the man said, twisting around to where Will stared. He spun to meet Will's gaze.

"Excuse me?"

"I see you watching that man intently." He twisted back, pointing at the helicopter blocking Will's view.

He has an accent. Iranian. I'm sure of it.

"Oh, no, I thought a rare bird flew by, is all. I do not know who you're talking about."

The man gave a stiff smile. A shoe scuff told him someone else had come onto the bridge from the other side. He looked over his shoulder. The man who had been with this guy earlier appeared.

Will stepped toward the first man. He didn't move.

"Where are you going?" The man asked. "The view is so nice up here."

His English is excellent. Maybe too good. As in state-trained men. He smiled at the man and tried to sidestep around him. The man moved to block him again.

What the hell! I can't risk a confrontation. Not when I'm so close to our target.

"My apologies, sir. If you'd allow me to pass, you can have the view all to yourself. I'd like to move on."

"Do you know those men?" The man asked, pointing out the window again.

The other man ignored the view. Instead, he crept up closer to Will from behind.

"Know who?"

The man smirked yet said nothing and stared hard at him.

Christ! Who the hell are these two?

"Are you an American?" The man asked.

"Yes, and I've got to be moving on. Now step aside, sir."

Distracted, Will lost track of the brothers.

They might be foreign agents. That seems a stretch, since they're supposedly unaware he fled, anyway.

Will felt a surge of adrenaline when the man grabbed his arm, realizing their intentions were not innocent. He jerked his arm away, pushed past the first man, and leaped toward the open hatch with steep stairs. He pointed his legs straight, tucked his elbows, and dropped through the opening, narrowly missing the steps as he flew down.

"Hey!" the man said after him.

He hit the next deck, rolling out of the fall with a somersault. As he came to his feet in one fluid motion, he heard the two men talking above. Will wasted no time, rushing down the passage to another hatch 30 meters away. The stairs behind him rattling metallically as the men rushed down.

I can't let them find out who I am. I also don't want them to get to Nafisi first. Have to lose them. Can't ID Nafisi with these goons around.

He slid down the rails of the next stairs. After landing on the deck with a thud, he immediately took off in the opposite direction as the floor above. Pounding footsteps overhead spurred him on.

A sign at this passageway's end showed the way back to the hangar. Will instead leaped over the chain across an opening with a red sign hanging in the middle that read, "Communications Room. Not Part of the Tour" in white engraved letters.

He crept silently through the space and emerged on the other side. The corridor there had no lights on, as it wasn't open to tourists. He paused against the wall, his heart thumping hard and fast.

Footsteps came down the stairs in the other passageway, revving up his heart again. They didn't linger, though, continuing down the stairs to the hangar. Will closed his eyes and focused on his breathing.

Who in the hell was that? Fuck! I've lost the brothers.

He remembered Jim. The icon in his virtual vision showed no connection. He had no bars inside this metal ship. Will wanted to confirm if he had obtained any images of these two men. When he checked, the connection had been spotty, and his glasses didn't get any facial recognition images. He thumped a fist on the wall and instantly regretted it, fearing his pursuers might've heard.

"Dammit."

His voice was a lonely sound in the dark, empty passageway. He was snapped back to the danger by the sounds of someone coming up the stairs.

Oh no! They heard me.

He peered with one eye around the corner through the communications room. On the other side, he glimpsed some school children climbing toward the flight deck. Their cacophony of voices reached him, and he relaxed, forcing himself to wait a few minutes longer until they passed.

Ten minutes later, he climbed down the stairs from the aircraft carrier's main elevator, knowing he'd failed miserably. The brothers had disappeared and the strange men were nowhere to be found.

For as long as I hid, they could've made it back to Iran.

Jim ran into him while ascending the stairs. "Boss! I lost comms with you. And I saw the brothers leave. Are you okay? Did they see you or something?"

"I'm fine. They didn't see me; I ran into an obstacle that kept me from keeping a visual on them. Come on. I'll explain in the car."

The pair took the stairs, side by side, and departed Patriots Point. Will was reticent, and Jim kept quiet, eyeing his leader a couple of times. They're all newbs led by a newb, a combination that usually ended badly.

No sooner did they leave the parking lot when Will got his cigarettes out of the center console. He offered one to Jim, who obliged by taking two, lighting them simultaneously. When he had them lit, he handed one over.

"We're not alone," Will said flatly.

His sudden declaration startled Jim, who began looking behind them and around the car. "What? Are we being followed? By who?"

"Not at the moment. We're not the only ones interested in the brothers. I think some people, probably Quds Force, are watching them too. I could tell by their features and accent. They seemed to know I was there watching the Nafisi's too."

"Oh, shit. Where are we going now?"

"We need to get back to Henry's." Will took a drag on his cigarette and wondered for a second about when he'd see Gabby again. "I wasn't expecting any interference from Quds Force. It appears that they've discovered Vahan's unexpected departure. Now we have to hustle."

VIII

Thursday, April 11, 1:25pm

Henry drove the drone crew from where he lived near Charleston's center, out to the west via highway 61. The suburbs came and went, dwindling to farms and untamed woods. The crew crammed the back of the minivan with containers, chairs, umbrellas, coolers, and computers.

Arnold rode shotgun, absorbed in his phone. The blimps and their helium tanks necessitated a second vehicle. John and Kevin followed in an Isuzu box truck. For immediate communications between the two, they used a pair of walkie-talkies.

Arnold suddenly picked up theirs from the center console and keyed its mic. "Kevin, son, I've found the perfect girl for you on Tinder."

Static emanated from the walkie before Kevin's tinny voice came through. "Oh, yeah? What are you talking about?"

"On Tinder, the pussy app."

"Oh, I see. Is my future wife Jewish, at least?"

"No, seriously. She's Jewish, of course, and wants a Jew husband from Israel, not America."

"I can't wait to see her," Kevin said, dropping the walkie back into the center console with an eye roll.

Henry turned to Arnold. "Why don't you scoop her up yourself if she's such a great catch?"

"Because I'm not interested in marrying. Someone like Kevin would be. He'll struggle getting any tail around here. This girl is cute. A few extra pounds. She'll take his virginity, and he will think he's found heaven."

Henry snorted, shook his head, and said, "Leave him alone. He's a good boy. Not a jaded asshole like you. Don't be the one who corrupts him."

"Corrupt? I want him to enjoy life. I can't help it. He annoys me with his perfect memory and bright eyes. It makes me wonder about having a little brother or apprentice. My real elder brother is a dumbass. I like the idea of having a brother who isn't a dumbass. You see what I mean?"

Henry thought about the founding fathers, Israel's rebirth, and the Institute. "Do you think that's what Ben-Gurion was talking about when they built Israel? Kevin isn't your little brother. He's a grown man, whose proven himself worthy of deserving to be here. By people ranked much higher than us."

"Why do you care what I do? I'm just saying I like the idea. You're taking it too seriously. I'll bet Ben-Gurion talked about fucking his girlfriend in the ass."

"You vile bastard! He was married and didn't have any perverted girlfriend. God's going to strike you down for saying such horrible things about an Israeli hero. He's a hero, like the Torah judges. Courageous and brave. Ruthless when he needed to be and cun—"

"And I'm sure he was as horny as Samson. And he didn't have a convenient dating app." He waggled his phone near Henry's face. "It might've saved him a lot of trouble. You see, I have this charm, good looks, and phone. Ben-Gurion would call me a fool if I wasted it."

The radio crackled. John said, "How much further? Are there women out there?"

Henry snatched the radio from the console before Arnold. "Ten or fifteen minutes and no, there are no girls there. It's a derelict farm."

Arnold asked, "A farm? Like with cows and goats?"

John's said, "How convenient. Arnold won't have trouble finding a date."

Henry flicked a hand in the air, glaring out the driver's window. He spun back toward Arnold. "You see. You are corrupting them already. I can't imagine Ben-Gurion talking this way. It's so vulgar!"

"Can you be any more of an old man?" An incredulous Arnold asked. "I mean, you're a man. You have desires. What about Yvette? Don't you two screw anymore?"

Henry remained silent. Arnold thought he might have taken it too far.

"Hey, I didn't mean—"

Henry waved off the idea and said, "No, no, it's not like that. Yvette is an operative like me. Like us. They offered her an assignment as the wife of another operative. We play the part and get along well enough. At first, we cared nothing for each other. Just pretending in front of others. Over time, more of something developed. Not some hot romance, mind you."

Suddenly, he raised his voice to a full lecture level. "We're here to work. For Israel! We'll never get put to the sword again, like lambs. The legacy left to us by our ancestors is to carry that torch. Remember that when you are risking the mission screwing around with tramps. Things matter; people matter. You risk exposing us and the mission. Frankly, I'd rather you turned off your phone before we got to the farm. Who knows who's tracking it? As a matter of fact—"

Henry picked the walkie-talkie up again and keyed it. "Listen, everybody, shut off your phones while we're out here. No exceptions."

"What about Will and Jim? What if they need help?" Kevin asked over the radio.

"John will be the only exception. He can listen up for them."

Henry set the radio down and pressed the brakes. They were approaching an unmarked dirt road. He steered onto it. Kevin and John followed. A massive plume of dust came from the minivan. Henry slowed to reduce the blinding cloud for the others behind.

The light-colored dirt road wound through the ever-present landscape of pine trees and palmetto bushes. It ended at a ten-acre clearing. At one end of the field stood a two-car garage house. A concrete driveway crossed the grassy area, leading to the garage on the right side of the house. They parked the van and truck in front of the garage. Everybody piled out and policed the area before taking bathroom breaks.

The blimp's many parts needed assembling. The resident experts, Kevin and John, wasted no time and began working as Henry and Arnold brought out a long cardboard box from the Isuzu truck. They carried everything around to the backyard. The back of the house had a screened-in porch.

"Why did we bring this tent if we have that?" Arnold asked. He pointed to the house's back. "That'll make an excellent command porch. Screw the tent; let's use that."

Henry scratched his head. "Well, it's been a while since I was out here last. Other operatives must have done some home improvements."

Arnold, carrying the tent on one shoulder, plopped it down next to the house and went to the porch. An orange extension cord snaked onto the patio through a window. "We've got power."

An hour later, they had the ten-meter-long blimps laid out, and the virtual reality rig set up. John had a cat ready to test. Kevin would start with a blimp as soon as one got inflated. Arnold manhandled a helium tank from the truck onto a dolly and rolled it out to where the blimp parts lay.

John initialized a cat and set it on the floor. He sat on one of the dusty wicker chairs and donned VR goggles. Blinded by the VR rig, he groped around on the table until he found the cat controller.

"Okay, I'm just waiting for sync confirmation. Oh, there it is. It looks like we're live. Okay, let's see what we can do."

The motionless cat suddenly sprang to life and nearly collided with the screen door.

"Aw, shit. This is weird to control at first. It's been a while since I did this. Lemme try backing it up."

The cat stepped backward a few paces. Henry opened the door and held it. The gray tabby dashed out, halted a few meters out, and scanned its surroundings.

John laughed out loud. "This is crazy! I can see great. And being able to move like this is amazing. A little disorienting."

Now he walked the cat toward the open field outback. As he got farther away, he increased the cat's speed until it ran at full tilt.

Arnold stepped up onto the porch, wiping his sweaty brow. "How's your pussy?"

John said, "Outstanding, but we're in a wide-open field. There are no buildings, trees, and cars blocking the signals. The telemetry feed and controls are very responsive out here. Put some trees and structures in the way, and it'll probably be sketchy." He pointed blindly toward the table. "Over there is a monitor you can turn on and see what I'm seeing."

Kevin came onto the porch from inside the house. He helped get the LED display patched into the system. After some fiddling, they got it working. Arnold stayed to watch John put the cat through its paces: running, walking, sitting, jumping up, jumping down, and crouching. Climbing isn't in these robots' repertoire; the maneuver was too complicated. Before he knew it, the thing needed a fresh battery.

They went out to the blimps lying ready to be filled with helium. Inflation requires all hands. John parked the cat near the porch and joined the others. Once the helium tanks had filled the gas chambers, he took over the cat controls with a fresh battery. Half an hour later, the first matte-black dirigible hovered a meter off the ground. John connected with a second computer and VR rig to control it.

Arnold, scratching at the back of his neck, asked, "How will you control four machines with just two people?"

"We can switch between units with the click of a button," Kevin said. "I can be flying the blimp and bam; a second later, I'm driving the cat. When we're not directly controlling them, they operate in autonomous mode."

Arnold's phone rang. "Ah! Maybe it's one of my ladies." He looked at his phone and frowned. "It's just Will."

Henry barked from outside. "Who's phone is that? I thought I said to turn them off."

Ignoring Henry, Arnold said, "Hello, Will, how are things? Is that so? Are you sure? Are you sure you saw Nafisi? Okay. Yes. No, we've seen nothing. All right, things are moving right along here. We'll see you back at the house. Relax. They probably thought you were Iranian. Oh, come on. Lighten up. Yeah, bye."

"What was that about?" John asked.

"Well, they positively ID'd the Nafisi brothers. I mean, Jim saw them both, and Will saw Hedyeh, likely with his brother. He had a run-in with some men. They were too nosey for comfort, or so he says. Now he thinks foreign agents are here too." Arnold rolled his eyes and spread his hands. "Jim never saw them, and Will lost track of them. And who fucking cares as long as we've got our target in our sights?"

Henry stomped onto the porch. "You should care. Never underestimate the little things. They always come back to bite you. I remember this one time—"

"Give it a rest, Henry. We've got a blimp to fly. I won't worry about Will's paranoia. Or yours, for that matter."

He turned to John and Kevin, who both sat on the wicker chairs now. One controlled a cat, and the other piloted a blimp. Arnold went outside with a grumbling Henry for the launch.

The blimp bobbed at skinny ropes leading from nose and tail to cinder block anchors. They detached the lines and held them, waiting for the blimp to rise or fall. Gradually, it ascended. Arnold tied off his rope and walked to the center of the dirigible. He picked a small sack filled with sand up from the grass he'd dropped there and stuffed it into the blimp's cargo hold.

That neutralized it just right. The cat and sack weigh about the same. They could remotely release helium to reduce buoyancy after deployment. He returned to his end and untied it. The turbofans kicked on, and the ropes slid from Henry and Arnold's hands as the black bulge rose into the air.

John took the blimp up to treetop level. It flew around the perimeter of the clearing like a majestic blackened cigar. When he'd made a full circuit, he brought it down to where the cinder blocks lay.

Kevin walked the cat to Arnold, who waited in the middle. He turned, picked the cat up, removed the sack of sand, and loaded kitty number one into the deployment compartment. The blimp bobbed and sank.

"Hang on," Arnold said. "I've got to add a little helium. How much helium do we have?"

Henry said, "Enough to fill four of these blimps. So plenty. Unless you waste it siphoning it off all day."

"Yeah, yeah, I'm not wasting it. Stand by; I'm giving it a squirt." He added a few seconds of helium. Satisfied, he cupped a hand to his mouth. "Okay, she's good. Casting off."

They detached the nose and tail lines again. John took the blimp up and held it stationary for several minutes on autopilot while he and Kevin worked out a plan to practice a cat deployment.

Henry and Arnold focused on the other blimp. After an hour, the daylight waned, and they still needed to test the second blimp, which floated ready for a maiden voyage.

Kevin took control of the second blimp, flying up and around the clearing. The wind picked up above the woods. They couldn't perceive the treetops swaying in the darkening sky.

The first blimp held stationary in autonomous mode, fifteen meters off the ground, roughly centered in the field. The black dirigible obvious, hanging there in the purple-and-orange sunset sky. Every few seconds, one of the twin turbines activated, keeping it in position.

Kitty number two came online. Prepped and tested by John without a hitch. When Kevin finished doing a shakedown flight of number two, he parked it in the sky near number one.

They let the others have a peek through the VR goggles. Arnold wanted to try piloting the blimp. Everybody vetoed that notion. Satisfied that both blimps and cats were ready, they ran through dropping-off-the-cat drills.

The cat could be released when the blimp reached a distance of three meters from the ground. The idea was for the cat to drop and land on its feet. They'd run it to the house and position it to spy through a window.

As the dusk eased into the evening, mosquitoes came out in force, and the team members smacked and swatted maniacally. Henry brought out some bug spray, and they all coated themselves. The katydids set off their racket, becoming loud enough that they had to raise their voices to be heard.

After John and Kevin did three drop-and-goes, circling the clearing and deploying a cat each, the group decided to call it a night. As they maneuvered the blimps for recovery, Kevin suddenly cried out.

"Shit!"

In the dark, he couldn't see. He misjudged his position relative to the trees, swung the tail wide, and caught a branch. The jolt and Kevin's knee-jerk reaction caused the blimp to spin around in the other direction.

RIIIIP

All eyes turned toward the ominous sound. A moment later, the flaccid black blimp plummeted out of the darkness. It landed in a ruined heap next to the other blimp, like a discarded condom.

IX

"What the fuck happened?" Arnold said, voice a angry growl. "Dammit, what happened?"

"I don't know! I was getting into position to land," Kevin said sheepishly. "And then—I don't know what happened. Maybe the wind caught it or something."

By now, Arnold had run upon the wreckage, protectively holding the other blimp's nose tether. "You fucking killed it," Arnold said. "You see? This highlights the problem I've got with this technology crap. It's always so fragile and temperamental."

He handed the rope to Henry, put on a headlight, and began picking up the black gas bag, searching for the payload section. When he found it, he lifted out the cat and brought it clear of the scrapped drone.

"How does it look?" Henry asked.

"We're about to find out," Arnold said. "Switch over to the bloody cat! Let's make sure this thing still works."

When he set the cat on the ground, it tipped over and fell on its side. "Kevin! The cat, son, check out the freaking cat!"

"I am!"

The cat jerked, wiggled its limbs, and gingerly got to its feet. Once it stood firm, Kevin swiveled the head back and forth, up and down. "Looks like it survived the crash," Kevin said.

Enraged by the destroyed blimp, Arnold stalked toward the house. When he reached it, he flung open the screen door with a resounding slap. "How could you crash the drone on a practice run?"

"It's not as easy as it looks," Kevin said as he gave control of the cat over to John and took off his VR goggles. "Are you synced, John?"

"Got it. Synced. Walking back now."

Kevin stood and headed for the exit. He brushed past Arnold, ignoring his teammate's fury. Dealing with hotheads is not something Kevin relished. Leaving the vicinity was his way of avoiding his father, who had been like that.

"You've cost us an asset," Arnold said.

Kevin kept his head low as he exited. "I'm sorry. It's dark, and the wind must have pushed me into the trees. I—"

"You weren't taking this shit seriously. You'd better get with the program. Where the hell are you going?"

Kevin, incredulous, said, "I'm not taking it seriously?" He kicked the screen door open. It flew wide, smacking into the wall. As he went through, he called over his shoulder. "You're the one who keeps fucking off on his phone all the time."

Arnold bristled at the jab and strode out after Kevin, who stomped along a few steps ahead. Arnold trotted after him and grabbed his arm. Kevin whirled, grabbed Arnold's wrist, and hauled him across his extended leg in a blur. Caught by surprise, Arnold tumbled to the ground with a grunt and crunch.

"Don't fucking touch me!" Kevin said, standing at the ready, back leg stabilized, arms poised for combat. He's a jujitsu black belt and can effortlessly defeat this loudmouth.

Arnold didn't get up immediately. Instead, he moaned, groaned, and rolled over, clutching at his left side. He turned his head. The beam showed behind him, revealing a crushed cat. "Son of a bitch," Arnold said.

Kevin said, "Aw, shit. Now a cat's crushed. You stupid idiot! Where do you get off thinking you can touch me?"

Arnold stared up at Kevin a second before attempting to get up. Holding his lower back, he reached out to Kevin with his other hand. "I think it got me in the kidney," Arnold said with a gasp.

"What? I'm not falling for that bullshit." Kevin remained on guard, assuming the sly old dog was trying to sucker him into letting his guard down.

By now, Henry had run to them. John burst out of the screen door moments later. John came to a halt over the damaged robot feline. "What happened? One second I was bringing the cat—" He saw it lit by their headlights at Arnold's feet. "How'd that happen?"

"Dumbass fell onto it," Kevin said.

"You fucking threw me onto it!"

"Hey, you two," Henry said. "That's enough. Shut up. Dammit, this is bad luck."

All of them stared at each other and the crushed cat. Arnold ran his hands through his hair. He bent over, picked the motionless cat up, and pulled off part of its fur coat, revealing a cracked carbon fiber frame. Wires torn from their sockets popped off a few sparks, and some other gizmo had a nasty dent in it. It wasn't even twitching. They killed a cat. It probably had a ninth life left. Unfortunately, they didn't have the parts or time to repair it.

Arnold heaved a deep sigh. "I'm sorry, guys. Shit, Will's going to have a duck." He scratched his head while he surveyed the field. "Well, there's nothing to be done about it. Let's get things picked up and loaded. I need a smoke."

He fished in his pocket and brought out his cigarettes and a lighter. As he lit up, John reached for the pack. Arnold handed it to him, and Kevin got one too. Everybody but Henry had a smoke break. Like mourners pausing over the news of a fallen comrade, they held a short vigil.

Arnold glared at Kevin, who glared back until Arnold broke the tension. "You know, son," he said with a smirk. "That was a smooth move you did on me. I didn't have a chance to even think about it. What is that? Judo?"

Kevin couldn't help grinning. It always felt good to throw a blowhard on his ass. "Jujitsu kicked in automatically. Sorry, man."

Arnold took a contemplative drag. "No, it's okay. I would've done the same thing. Only faster and harder." He gave a pompous sniff and tugged on the waist of his pants. "You're good with those reflexes. It makes me wonder if I'm over the hill."

Kevin frowned and nodded. "And when I screw up, like just now, I wonder if I'm too much of a klutz to be doing this stuff." He kicked at the grass idly.

Arnold sighed, then said, "It happens. I'm not even going to tell you about some of my fuck-ups from back in the day."

They chuckled together.

"Let's get moving. I'm tired and want a hot shower. I just wanted you to know—I mean, I shouldn't have bitten your head off and all..."

Kevin gave him a few seconds to finish. Arnold said nothing more; instead, he took a drag on his cigarette.

"I can't say it's all right, but I understand. We all get angry. I screwed up, and it pissed you off. We reacted. Now we have a dead cat and a flaccid blimp." More chuckles. "Maybe we should all relax and get focused."

Arnold nodded, flicked his cigarette butt away, and slapped him on the back. "Let's get out of here."

He and Kevin helped the team gather their things and leave. By the time they pulled into Henry Banks' garage at 1:35 a.m. Everybody wanted one thing: sleep. Having waited up, Will ordered the team to stay the night at the Banks' home. He didn't get as much flack as he expected over the idea.

At first, he thought they were all exhausted, given their long faces. Understanding dawned after they confessed to destroying a blimp and cat. Aggravated, Will had to admit that Arnold might have a point about technology.

More trouble than it is worth, it seems. Tomorrow will be a new day. The mission is progressing. Some setbacks. Nothing to stop us at this point.

Earlier, he made an inquiry to the Israeli Institute about known state entities operating in Charleston. Before bed, he checked for a reply message and found none. He called it a night and turned in with everybody else.

<u>X</u>

Friday, April 12, 6:45am

Five hours later, Will awoke on a bed in one of the upstairs bedrooms, still dressed. Sunlight showed through the window. A familiar odor cracked his eyes open a little wider. *Coffee. Thank God.*

The rest of the team trickled down from upstairs, taking seats at the small dining table or perching on barstools. The bar separated the kitchen and dining room. Arnold sat at the table in a black terry-cloth robe with a coffee, phone in hand, and reading glasses perched on his nose. John and Jim hunched over their coffee at the bar, clothes unchanged from the day before. Yvette toiled away in the kitchen, making breakfast.

As Will came down the stairs, he caught the tail end of a conversation.

Jim said, "Yeah, I had to go find him once I saw the brothers leave. I thought he'd seen a ghost on the Yorktown, the way he looked. Then he was all silent and weird..."

He trailed off when Will entered. Awkwardness gripped the room.

Criticizing me already? I don't think I looked that scared. Did I?

Floorboards creaked behind him as Henry came down, shoes in one hand.

Will shuffled straight to the coffeepot. He croaked, "Good morning, everyone."

A few moans and groans greeted him in return. Nobody slept well. Henry stopped on the landing, sitting to put his shoes on.

Arnold glanced up from his phone, sipped coffee, and set the cup down with a clink. "Why in the hell are you panicking?"

In the kitchen, Will, preparing his coffee, closed his eyes for a moment. *Thanks, Arnold, for not wasting any time getting into the shit.* With a sigh, Will said, "Panicking?"

"Yeah, about those mystery men."

"What are you talking about? I'm not panicking. Those men are agents. I'm sure of it. I'm concerned for you, and my safety is all."

Yvette said, "Well, wouldn't you be safe in your hotels? You could all go there right now. I wouldn't mind one bit."

Will came out of the kitchen, leaned on the bar, and had a sip of coffee before speaking. "I'm sorry for the inconvenience. When our cover was intact, things were different. Now that others may suspect our presence, I can't overlook that risk."

"Our covers aren't blown," Arnold said. "Besides, I can look after myself. We don't need to circle the wagons at the drop of a hat."

Will felt the siren call of nicotine. "Jumping right into it straight off, eh?"

"I'm not 'jumping straight into it,'" Arnold said. "I slept like shit last night on the couch while you were snug in a bed. I'm not staying here again tonight." He clinked his cup down hard on its saucer.

Will sipped at his cup and swallowed. "We'd have a problem. I'm the lead. I've given an order. What is unclear about all of this? If you don't like how things are going, we can make a conference call to the Institute."

The others remained silent as a sudden chill seized the room.

Arnold smirked and shook his head. He said nothing more and returned to his phone.

Henry stood up, walked behind Arnold, and placed his hands on his shoulders. "Arnold, brother, I'm sorry if you were so uncomfortable on the couch. I often fall asleep on that thing, so I thought you would too. It's a nice couch. It's a good couch. If you need a bed, you may take mine, and I will sleep on the couch tonight."

Arnold sighed. He patted one of Henry's hands and smiled back at him. "I'll be fine. Thank you. I couldn't put you out of your bed. Toda Rába, brother."

Henry squeezed his shoulders one last time before moving to the kitchen.

"I'll take a neck rub," John said.

Henry obliged and gave him a quick massage of the neck where he sat hunched at the bar.

Jim said, "I'll take a hand job."

Henry jabbed a finger into Jim's head. Laughing, Jim had to lean away.

"You see! You had to ruin it. Today's generation has no respect," Henry said.

Chuckles floated around the room. Will noticed Yvette shaking her head, busily preparing breakfast. The sight made him think of Gabriella.

Not that Gabby is much of a homemaker. He couldn't help thinking of her face, body, and voice. *Damn, I miss her.*

Will asked, "Yvette, what's on the menu this morning? Do you need any help?"

"Oh, toda, Will. I've got my way of doing things. You'd only get in the way."

"Okay, let me know if you do."

They ate a buffet straight out of the cooking pans and pots using paper plates. The fare was eggs, berries, hash browns, and waffles with pecans in them. It tasted like breakfast on a holiday morning. All they wanted to do was nap afterward. Will agreed, telling them to reconvene at noon. They'd prepare the remaining blimp in the evening.

For the rest of the morning, Kevin loafed around the house, brooding. Meanwhile, John kept an obsessive eye on wind and weather forecasts. Arnold nursed a sore back. Jim wrecked the bathroom several times throughout the day because of something he'd eaten in Africa. Henry bitched endlessly about the Wi-Fi slowing down and screwing up his soccer game. Yvette fumed because five guests dropped in on her unannounced. As for Will, he felt content, knowing they're all here, safe and sound.

XI

As the sun set that Friday evening, around nine, Will retreated to the rooftop patio alone. A long day was spent preparing. With a single blimp and cat, everything needed to go right, and a more subdued team worked well this afternoon to hone their skills.

He felt the urge to further investigate the mystery men by searching through a vast dossier collection of known operators, which was compiled by the Mossad. *Damn. They all look alike: angry and bearded. These men I encountered were only a day or two out from a clean shave, though.* He saw some possibilities. Nothing for sure. *Maybe Arnold is right: It's nothing, and I'm just paranoid.*

He knew the men were state officers, posing a potential mission compromise. His team might head into a trap. On the flip side, the Mossad agents are now aware of their presence.

They've tipped their hand. I'm sure they're as concerned as we are about the unknown. Not to mention operating on foreign soil. How much intel could they have? Surveillance? We need to have a look at and listen in on the Nafisi's. I believe we can still do this.

His phone vibrated on the table. He picked it up to view the notification from headquarters in response to his inquiry.

'Negative to abort. Proceed with package pickup.'

He got up from the table to let the others know about the extended stay. Tonight, they'd run a surveillance mission. It'll set them up for a snatch and grab the next night.

When he laid it out to the team, Arnold tried to argue that they should use tried-and-true physical surveillance. Again, Will overruled him.

"One blimp and one cat are still in play. Until they're unavailable, we'll try our best to do all of this at arm's length until it's time to capture Nafisi."

The agents remained indifferent about the decision. Subconsciously, they all felt exhilaration building for an unfolding chase and caper.

The Isuzu box truck is big enough to hold everything needed to fly the blimp. Ten helium tanks got wrestled into the back and strapped to one side. Half of them were empty now. A workbench spanned the opposite wall from front to back.

Will and Henry are to crew it during flight ops, serving as a command post. Should the blimp go down, they'd act fast and retrieve it. The blimp wasn't much of a security risk. However, the cat used technology that wasn't common—therefore; they must recover it at all costs.

Tonight, though, the truck sat inside the Banks' oversized garage. Earlier today, a local friend of the Institute wrapped the cargo box with plastic. The outside now advertised 'Two Dudes and a Truck Movers.'

It took the entire team to clear off the Banks' roof patio, layout, and assemble the blimp. When the bag reached full inflation, one had to stand at the patio edge. Its nose and tail secured to cinder blocks at each end. John stood on the stairs at liftoff for lack of room.

Once it cleared, Kevin set up the table with two chairs for him and John to use while wearing the VR goggles. He'd copilot for now until it's time to deploy the remote controlled robot. Once the cat was loose, he'd drive it.

After helping with the blimp, Arnold, Yvette, and Jim went back to the farm. They prepared the house to hold Nafisi until they got him exfiltrated. Preparation comprised emptying a bedroom, leaving a stripped mattress, and boarding up the window. They also flipped the doorknob around. Its lock faced outward now. Once a guest occupied the makeshift holding cell, the locking mechanism would be convenient on the outside.

The trio practiced a range of skills, including driving fast, stopping abruptly, breaking into doors, picking locks, entering the house, and capturing Nafisi. Yvette took part by playing the part of the scientist. They also practiced shooting their way into the building. Arnold had them practice as many scenarios as they could conceive.

That evening, fortune smiled on them, giving a moonless, clear night with a slight breeze. Which also meant hot and muggy, with little wind to circulate things.

"Bird's-eye is airborne," John said.

Blackened for stealth, the blimp is a shadow against the backdrop of stars.

No matter what direction it faced, two tiny directional antennas on its underside stayed pointed toward the house. They streamed its control telemetry and video data back in a tight beam to a small, motorized directional antenna mounted on a pole. It rose ten meters above the house, tracking the blimp by rotating or inclining the dish. After liftoff, Kevin raised the antenna back up and sat at the table.

In the dark, neither the blimp nor the antenna are visible. John took it up as rapidly as he dared. At twenty meters, one lost sight of the bulging wraith. Around fifty meters, the whir of its fans became undetectable. At one hundred meters, he turned the blimp toward the Nafisi home for a four-kilometer trip through the humid night.

Will and Henry sat in the truck's cargo hold on stools, backs to the workbench, watching the monitors mounted to the wall above the helium tanks. A moving blanket that hung above the monitors kept them hidden from plain sight when not in use. Will rolled it up to reveal the LED screens and secured it in place with Velcro straps.

Printouts, hand tools, laptops, coffee mugs, circuit cards, soda cans, and paper plates covered the bench. A three-centimeter lip on the workbench prevented items from rolling off during truck movement.

The blimp had one 360-degree digital camera for still shots and video. It looked in all directions of a hemisphere at once, digitally manipulating the image to simulate multiple cameras. One monitor showed the blimp view, and another showed the cat's stereo perspective.

Stereo vision permitted a person to have depth perception while maneuvering it. The word 'Hibernating' blinked in white letters on a black background. A third monitor had readouts of the blimp and cat telemetry.

After digesting all the information, Will felt reasonably confident in their equipment. *I'm not sure where we'll capture Dr. Nafisi—either the house or the business. Maybe on the street. It could be a while before he develops a pattern in his daily movements we can exploit. The workplace probably has a regular schedule. Hopefully, its owner gets in early or stays late with his brother. We'll see.*

John's voice came through Will's Bluetooth earbuds. "Can you check the map? I'm following this road, and now I'm confused. I don't want to go too far out of the way. We only have so much battery power."

"Standby."

Newer versions of the blimps had built-in GPS trackers. This one lacked the update.

"Why in the hell didn't they make the GPS visible in VR?" John said.

"I read a bulletin that says a new firmware package coming out will have GPS," Kevin said.

John attempted to memorize the routes beforehand; otherwise, he followed roads to navigate. Sometimes, neither technique worked.

"You're very close," Will said. "Turn to two, seven, zero, and go maybe three hundred meters. At that point, you should about be over the intersection that's near his house."

A moment of silence. John's breathing pulsated softly through the communications line. Except for Arnold, Yvette, and Jim, the others were in the same conference call using earbuds and Android phones to communicate.

"Yeah, got it. Bringing her around. Okay, back on course. Looking for the intersection."

Below, homes and widely spaced streetlights spread out half a kilometer in all directions. There's minimal traffic and few pedestrians at this hour.

"There's something up ahead. Yes, it's a gas station. I'm coming down in altitude some for a better look. One, two, three—the fifth house, right? The backyard is dark. It looks like nobody's outside. Okay, I'm in position above the house. Ready for a blackout."

The 360-degree digital camera allowed the imagery to split into multiple views. John could focus on flying ahead, while another person looked behind using a separate data link. That included directly below.

"No, no, it's the next house over."

"Are you sure?" John said.

"Yes. It's one house over. To the northeast."

"Okay, okay. So, this one?"

A small, green arrow appeared over a house on their monitors. Will scrutinized the image.

That's Hedyeh's house, all right. There's the driveway, fence, bushes, and the Jetta.

"Standby."

Will nodded affirmation to Henry, who picked up a smartphone and sent a text. Their hacker contact is someone he can contact once per phone. The burner phone is only good for one time. Henry keeps a tackle box with several of them ready to go.

Their contact is the paranoid sort. The hacker has all kinds of back doors into the various county government computer systems. Besides that, he's into the power grid. That particular access is what they needed tonight.

"That's the right house. Stand by where you're at; we're waiting for our friends to give us some cover. Be ready to move."

"Roger that."

Kevin and John sat ready at the patio table. Kevin asked, "How does she feel?"

"Excellent. Very stable in this still air. It makes it easy to control. Telemetry looks good."

"I really don't know what happened," Kevin said, thinking back. "The trees reached out and hit me, I think."

"Don't beat yourself up," Will said. "It could've happened to any of us. We're just lucky we had two, and the luxury of a practice run."

"He's right, you know," John said. "Shit happens. Don't forget—this is about protecting Israel, not your pride."

"I know. I just can't believe I did that. It seems like such a screwup. It nearly scrubbed the entire mission."

Henry chuckled. "It'll wear off after a while, son. We accept our faults and move on. Lesson learned." Henry received a text comprising a smiling cat, GIF, with glowing demon eyes. "I think that means yes. What's the blimp seeing?"

"Bird's-eye, seeing anything yet?"

After a few seconds, John said, "There it goes! Power's out. Black as pitch in this neighborhood now. Taking her down for deployment."

They saw the same blackness suddenly blot out their monitors. Night vision compensated within seconds. They had visuals again. On the telemetry screen, the altimeter decreased.

"Roger that. We're watching. Kevin, are you ready?"

"Yeah, the cat is coming out of standby now. Okay, it's ready to deploy."

"I'll tell you when it's a good time," John said. "Hang tight."

"Roger that."

On the monitors, they viewed the backyard of the house from fifty meters up, looking straight down. Will switched the view to thermal.

There are at least five people inside. Two of them appear to be in bed. Probably kids. The rest are in the kitchen and living room. "Nobody's reacting weirdly to the power outage on thermal. Proceed."

The night vision aiming below showed a yard filled with clutter. A car with a tarp over it. A partially dismantled lawnmower. A dilapidated shed. Other unidentifiable debris lying around.

At least there are no dogs. I can't see any doghouse, bowls, or well-trod paths around the yard.

Will couldn't imagine these people would take proper care of an animal given the yard's disarray. And that's fine with him. He noticed his palms sweating and rubbed them on his pants.

Henry glanced at him. "Nervous?"

Will raised his eyebrows without looking at him, keeping his eyes on the monitors. "Well, aren't you? This is nerve-racking crap. Of course, I'm nerv—John, that spot over there."

The blimp stopped descending, shimming over a meter. On target, John resumed the descent. "Yeah, I see it too… just getting her eased in… okay, Kevin, I'm one meter off the deck. You're green for release."

The camera jerked, stabilizing quickly. Now the image appeared to rise from the ground.

"Cat's away!" Kevin said. "I'm on the ground. System's check, okay. Bird's-eye, lemme know if it's safe to move."

"Roger that. The cat's away. The yard is still clear. Home base?"

"All souls in the house remain indoors. They're milling around in the blackout. I don't think they've noticed the drop. Kevin, you're on your own from here on out. John, take Bird's-eye to one hundred meters and hold station as communications relay until we hack their Wi-Fi."

Kevin used the cat's night vision to creep up to the house. Its ear microphones picked up the commotion inside. Naturally, the power outage puzzled and annoyed the people there. The air conditioning wasn't running because the windows were open, letting in what little breeze buffeted the night.

Suddenly, the back door creaked open, and Hedyeh stepped outside. Kevin backed the cat away and had it sit down in the shadows. They watched Hedyeh light a cigarette. A second man emerged as the door opened again. It's Vahan Nafisi.

"There's our man," Will said. "Henry, how much long—"

The video stream from the cat flared white when the back porch light ignited like a supernova. The electricity couldn't stay off long, or it would draw too much attention. Hedyeh turned, saw the cat, and called to it.

Kevin said, "Uh-oh, I think he's seen me."

XII

"A cat! Vahan, look, a cat. Psst, Psst, here, kitty," Hedyeh said in Persian as he stepped toward it. "Come here, kitty. I won't hurt you."

Jim, fluent in Persian, asked, "Is everybody up on their Persian? He's talking to his brother about the cat."

"I suck at Persian. I gathered that's what he was saying, though," Kevin said, tongue poking from the corner of his mouth as he drove the cat.

"How can you not know some Persian?" Will asked. "I've gotten rather good at it myself. Most of our missions are connected to Iran lately."

Hedyeh took another step toward the cat, hand stretched out. Kevin stood the cat up, turned it around, and walked into the shadowy, cluttered backyard.

The rest of the crew held their breath.

Hedyeh took only a few more steps. Thinking he had scared it away, he returned to the porch and resumed his smoke. Kevin posted the cat where it had a view from behind a pile of old tires.

Sounding tinny and distant through the cat's ears, Vahan asked, "What do you think happened to the electricity? Does it go out often here? Is that your neighbor's cat or something?" He paused his barrage of questions and leaned on the railing. "I don't like cats. I guess it doesn't like us either. Maybe it only knows English? Or it doesn't like the smoke. You're too old to be smoking those things, by the way."

"I'm also too old to hear your shit. You're full of all kinds of curiosity tonight, eh?" Hedyeh asked with a huff of cigarette smoke.

Vahan sighed and stepped away from the smoke plume. John snapped night-vision pictures of him from the blimp.

Kevin said, "I'm picking up Wi-Fi again. It looks like the strongest one is theirs. Cracking the key. It might be a few minutes."

"Okay," Will said, "get closer, though. Their voices are faint."

Kevin cautiously brought the cat out from around the tire pile and crept closer to the brothers chatting on the porch. He stayed in the shadows and settled close. With the cat sitting still, he focused its ears on the conversation. They swiveled and honed in on the sounds.

Vahan's voice became loud and clear. "... your wife cooks better these days. She's learned a lot since I last saw her. Back then, she could ruin boiled water."

"I've noticed the improvement myself." Hedyeh patted his third-trimester belly with a chuckle. "She's a persistent woman and spent a lot of time watching YouTube videos about cooking."

"Ah, the government censors the internet heavily back home. I can't even get to the website, let alone watch any videos."

"That's a shame. It's beneficial for learning. Lots of it is a waste of your brain cells, though. It's embarrassing to think of how many cat videos I've watched. I'll show you tomorrow at work. Speaking of which, the freight driver called and said he'd be there around 5:00 p.m. tomorrow to deliver thirty-two machines. So, we'll have to clear some room in the warehouse to fit them inside somehow."

Will looked at Henry, raising his eyebrows. "There's our chance."

Vahan said, "I'm actually looking forward to doing something menial. When my colleagues got murdered, I knew I had to leave. Two of my friends got killed by magnetic bombs attached to their cars, you know. It scared me to death, Hedyeh. It was horrible, just horrible." He shivered and shook his head. "Well, I guess you know, when Siemens sent me an invitation to attend the symposium on nuclear energy in Germany, I knew that was my way out. So, I don't care if we're picking up garbage around here; it sounds relaxing in comparison. I'm happy to be here with my brother and his family. I believe Allah is smiling on us."

Vahan reached out and patted his brother on the shoulder.

"Yes, we don't feel so alone here in America with at least one family member nearby now." " Hedyeh took a drag on his cigarette and blew it out. "We'll get you a place of your own, eventually. To do that, we have to make some money. So, we'll be at work late tomorrow night, but we don't have to go in until lunchtime. We've also got to get you a work visa and--"

"We will, we will, brother. There's no rush. I'm here, and all will be well. I just want to lie low for a while. Let my nerves calm down. Do something mundane and out of the limelight."

"Those Quds Force thugs can't get you here," Hedyeh said with a dismissive wave.

"They can get me anywhere," Vahan said with a frown. "Don't fool yourself. That being said, I don't feel so important. My supervisors hardly seemed to notice I was there at Natanz. With Allah watching over me, I gave them the slip, though." He shrugged. "I have time to hide. Fade away. Long enough to be ready for them, at least. There's no way anyone knows where I am at the moment. I'm supposed to be in Germany. That's a long way from here. Colder too. Did you know, at my last security interview, they still thought you lived in Canada? I didn't bother to correct them. So I doubt they've even realized I left."

"That's good, brother. I've been anxious about you with the assassination stories. How are you with bookkeeping?"

"Bookkeeping? Hedyeh, I'm a scientist, not a secretary. I don't know the first thing about counting beans."

Hedyeh grinned and dropped his cigarette on the wooden porch. "I was just asking." He put it out with his shoe. "Seeing what my new employee knows."

"Like I was saying, anything is better than where I came." With a sigh, Vahan said, "So I guess I can learn to count beans."

As Will listened to their conversation, he couldn't help pangs of guilt. The Nafisi brothers went back inside to resume watching a soccer match.

These men don't seem like bad people. It sounds like Nafisi isn't very passionate about what he was doing. We all get roped into things we don't expect.

Will thought it'd be best for the team to settle into a surveillance routine for a few weeks, considering the Nafisi brother's apparent stability. Learning their patterns allows for easy pickup at any time. They had the upper hand and could carefully orchestrate the kidnapping.

Maybe headquarters wouldn't want Dr. Nafisi anymore, and they'd simply keep tabs on him? Why would they send us here to grab him in the first place? And those men. I'm forgetting they're lurking out there somewhere. As of right now, he's our target, and nothing has changed. A few days ago, he was helping Iran build nuclear weapons. Getting cold feet doesn't absolve him, nor does it make what he knows worthless. One thing's for sure—we can't let Iran acquire nuclear weapons. I hate it for you, Nafisi, but when it comes down to it, you're coming with us at some point. The sooner we're done here, the sooner I can return home to Gabby.

Kevin interrupted his thoughts. "Okay, I'm into the network. Cat is connected. John, I've killed the Bird's-eye link."

"Roger that, Kevin. John, bring Bird's-eye home."

"Roger that, heading home."

The stealth-blimp fan motors spun to life. As it drifted away, Will noticed people in the video feed. "Stop! John, hold that position. There's a car parked out front that wasn't there earlier. I think I saw someone in it. Come back and down some."

John brought the blimp down to thirty meters and stopped over the street. A white Chevy Cruze sat idle, parked one house down from the Nafisi residence.

Using thermal imaging, they observed two men sitting inside.

Will had a hunch these were the same men he'd encountered at the Yorktown. "Bring the cat around the front and see if you can get a look. They're in a small white sedan. You can't miss it. They're the only ones out there at the moment."

"On it." The cat's view jiggled and swayed.

Will's phone vibrated—it's Arnold. He answered, adding him to the conference call. Background noise and indistinguishable voices came over the line before Arnold said, "Hello? Hey, boys, how's it going?"

"We're in the middle of something. What do you have?"

"The safe house is all set, and we're on our way back. How's our future guest doing?"

"He's looking forward to a new life here in America. They're at Hedyeh's home. You're on a conference call with everybody else, so maintain comm-discipline."

"What's our status?"

"Cat's at the henhouse. Bird's-eye is flying home shortly. So far, so good. All lights are blinking green. I've got a feeling our mystery men from the Yorktown showed up. We're moving into position to ID some people in a car parked out front."

"Whoa, drama already," Arnold said.

"We'll see, stand by." Kevin maneuvered around to the front yard. Leaves and gravel crunched like someone chewing on the phone, modulated by motor noise as the cat padded along. It hopped the neighbor's chain-link fence, then crossed the driveway and front lawn. He got to within two meters of the car, taking cover behind a skinny palm tree.

"I can't make out their faces. See if you can find a better angle."

"That's the best you'll get, boss. It's open grass all around except this one part with a scrawny tree. If a car comes by, we'd probably get a flash of their faces."

A vehicle backed out of a nearby driveway and directed itself towards the Chevy Cruze on cue. The passing car didn't hurry, shining light into the Cruze for a few seconds.

Displays washed out.

When they cleared, two men materialized. Will stared at the monitor a second before turning to Henry. "It's them."

"Who's them?" Arnold said from the speakerphone.

"The ones from Yorktown—the guys I had a run-in with. They're parked out front of Hedyeh's house as we speak."

"Well, shit, I guess you were right. Okay, I'm putting you on speaker, too, so the others can hear this."

Rustling sounds and murmured voices came over the line as Arnold plugged his phone into the van's USB port. The sound's tone changed. "There, now everyone in the van can hear. What's this about seeing your boyfriends?"

Will said, "Dammit, Arnold, this isn't a game. I'm telling you that other agents are at work here."

"All right, all right, don't get your bloomers in a knot. I'm just fucking with you. I don't have a visual to look at. Do you think cat-boy can get a pic of the license plate? And send it to us to look up?"

"Shit, I should've thought of that," Kevin said under his breath.

Kevin captured facial images through the fence, then he inspected the fence for an opening. Finding nothing convenient, he positioned the cat and made it leap over the fence. It tumbled into a quick corrective maneuver, rolling onto its feet behind the car, where it lowered into a crouch.

After a glance under the car, he stood the cat up. Failing to focus for a few seconds, he stepped back until the license plate became clear, then took some pictures.

"All right, get clear. Back to the other side of the fence."

Kevin executed a cleaner hop, landing smoothly on all fours. He took it to the tree and paused. The car's dome light came on as the passenger exited.

"What's he doing?" Henry asked.

The man closed his door quietly, standing still for a moment. From this vantage point, the cat had a clear shot of his feet.

"I don't know. Probably snooping around," Will said with a shrug.

John zoomed in on the man. He looked around frequently as he walked. The man surveyed the driveway entrance.

If he glanced the cat's way, he'd see it behind the tree. Kevin moved, covering behind the tree

They watched him creeping up the driveway, constantly checking windows and his surroundings. The Quds Force man stepped close to a window. He tried looking through cracks in the curtains. Apparently unsuccessful, he skulked around to the back.

"Hold steady, everybody."

"What's going on?" Arnold asked.

"One man in the car got out and approached the house. He's snooping around. Doing the same thing we are, really, without a robot cat or blimp."

Will worried about what the man might attempt to do behind the house when he suddenly came jogging back down the driveway. The man didn't give the impression of running away from something as much as trotting back to exchange a few words with the other man. Satisfied, he re-entered the car, and they drove off.

"What are they up to? Whatever it is, we've got to move quick."

One hundred meters above, John turned the blimp in pursuit. Immediately, the blimp's battery indicator turned red. He broke off the chase before it even began.

Meanwhile, Kevin maneuvered the cat to a power outlet in the messy shed behind Hedyeh's house. One of the cat's front paws spread and opened to reveal a plug that he inserted for a recharge. Battery level read ninety-five percent. He left it in autonomous mode to top off the battery.

With the blimp en route and no battery to spare, Kevin hastily moved their gear and cleared the patio. Conditions remained calm. They weren't expecting anything too complicated. As long as its batteries held out.

"Come on, come on, baby," John said like a mantra. "Just a few hundred more meters and you're home. Don't die yet. Come to papa."

All that remained on the patio now were John and his plastic chair. His forearms rested on the chair's arms while his hands held a wireless controller.

Will and Henry emerged from the stairway, ready to retrieve Bird's-eye.

"Okay, I'm right over the house. Descending."

After a moment, they heard faint fan noise getting louder. They spread out on the patio and craned their necks in search of the blimp. Another minute or two passed before any of them caught a glimpse. Through the hazy night air, at around twenty meters up, it hove into view.

John shut off the fans and bled some helium. The dark bulge loomed as it lowered close enough for Kevin to jump and grab a line dangling from the nose. He pulled it down, and Henry helped while Will grabbed the rear cord, and together they hauled it in like a black whale they'd harpooned.

In the closing moments of the landing, John scrambled clear to the side, shoving his goggles up. They tied it off and opened its purge valve. Helium gushed for the next half hour while everyone made their way to the garage. Arnold, Jim, and Yvette pulled in with the minivan a minute or two later.

Cigarettes got passed out, and they all took turns watching the replays from the cat and blimp video feeds, using the monitors in the truck. When they'd seen enough, all felt a decision needed making.

"Okay, so some goons are following Nafisi," Arnold said. "No real surprise there. He's a runaway scientist. I say we watch them, too. Maybe we can find out something interesting about them."

"No," Will said with a hand chop. "Let's stay focused on our scientist. We'll end up losing track of him while we diddle around playing cat and mouse with other agents. However, I'm not opposed to putting a tracking device on them if we get a chance. Passively keeping track of them couldn't hurt. Especially now since we may abort the mission."

"Aborting it? For what?" Arnold said incredulously.

"Yeah, why would we abort?" Jim asked.

Yvette said, "We'll have gone through all this and crammed you all into my house for nothing. There's never any hot water since you five moved in, by the way. No peace, no quiet. You can't quit now."

Will folded his arms and walked back and forth in the garage. "There's too much risk of engaging these men. If we can ID them as Iranian agents, they can probably do the same for us. The repercussions could be severe. For instance, how did we know Nafisi would be here? They might extrapolate where they have a leak, exposing our people inside Iran. We must be fast and careful if we go through with it."

Arnold climbed into the truck's back to see for himself. He took a few seconds before approaching the edge of the truck cargo area, panning his gaze across the crew. "They definitely look Iranian," he said with a glance over his shoulder. "We should hear something back soon from the Institute, right?"

Will shrugged and shook his head, expressing his uncertainty of a speedy reply.

Arnold frowned and said, "Well, hopefully, they can identify them and give us some actual information. I think we're in too deep to abort. Iranian fuckheads or not. Let's get this Jew-hating asshole and get out of here."

Henry said, "I agree."

Will ran a hand through his hair. "All right, we won't abort—under one condition. We move the timetable up to tomorrow night for a grab at the workplace."

Somebody gasped, and all heads turned to Will.

"That's one extreme to the other," Arnold said as he hopped down from the truck.

"If we delay, those guys might get him." Will glanced at Yvette. "And we would've done all of this for nothing. They may be here to kill him. And it may all be an elaborate hoax to get Nafisi into an American government nuclear facility. We know where he'll be, and the office park is a ghost town after sunset. They said they'd be there until at least nine tomorrow night."

Kevin folded his arms. "That works for me. I'd prefer getting it over with rather than waiting around for a long time. I'll bet these other guys won't be expecting it either."

Henry nodded. "Seems crazy and brazen. I like the odds, though. We could have Nafisi out of the country by Monday morning."

"Are you sure?" Arnold asked. "I didn't mean for us to get hasty. If you really want to take our time, we can. You're the lead, so it's up to you. I'm merely playing devil's advocate."

"Yeah, I'm sure," Will said, nodding. "The more I think about it, the better it sounds. And you're right, Kevin, they won't be expecting it. We'll take the truck and minivan, break into the office, kidnap the doctor, and whisk him away. It might upset Hedyeh that his new employee is leaving so soon, but we'll have our prize. If there are no real objections, I'm going to call it a night. In the morning, we'll put the plan together and have a rehearsal in the afternoon."

Everybody unconsciously looked at Arnold, who noticed the stares. The plan hinged on his tacit approval. He cleared his throat before answering. "Yeah, I'm up for some regular guns and fists. No more of this video game bullshit."

"Right then, let's get some rest. We've got a busy day ahead."

XIII

Saturday, April 13, 7am

The team hammered out a plan the next morning over coffee. For starters, John and Kevin would recover the deployed cat. That was a simple process of getting close, opening the van's sliding door, and walking it inside.

Yvette, for once, was in a giddy mood. The idea they'd all move out soon put a spring in her step. She, Arnold, and Jim made a field trip to a local Walmart for some dark clothing. Yvette volunteered to take them, since she needed extra groceries, anyway. They both got black jeans and black T-shirts and stopped at a military surplus store for tactical gloves to complete the ensemble.

Kevin and John brought back a smashed and dead cat. Someone discovered it in the Nafisi's shed and stomped its head. When they checked the video stream recordings, they glimpsed a man bringing his foot down on the cat before it went black. The man bore a striking resemblance to the Quds Force agents.

It sent a chill through the team. The game was afoot. It was more than afoot—they'd fucked with a cat.

Will might call himself anxious while others would say "nervous." Either way, his sweaty palms, armpits, and fidgeting annoyed him now, as it always had. He worried about hitting the wall and being unable to continue during his early training. Some studies came easily to him, like learning Persian. Physical training and focusing on survival brought fits of tension.

During that period, his body betrayed his anxiety every day with embarrassing perspiration when there was no physical activity. As time went on, he watched cadet after cadet get disqualified from the training group. Despite his outward signs of tension, it didn't affect his functioning.

My worst training instructor, Sergeant Cohen, made sure of that. He's the fairest and most even-tempered person I've ever met. While being the most sadistic masochist drilling young Israel Defense Forces kids. No matter the crisis, he knew how to lead us through it. He always knew what to do. It didn't stop the bastard from picking on me for my wet armpits.

As time went on during training, he discovered how autonomous one's body can be. A vivid fantasy can trigger the body's counter-mechanisms. And when you know that, you can ignore those autonomic functions—mind over matter. However, he wasn't running through the Negev playing war games. He's in a real covert operation with genuine consequences. Naturally, his armpits perspired as he typed out a message asking permission to modify their timeline and sequence of events.

That afternoon, Will posted himself alone on the patio with his laptop open, alternating between it and his phone. He searched local dating sites posing as a female looking for someone to 'enjoy sunsets, football, and hikes' within the off-chance one of the Quds Force men would turn up. The weirdo responses were becoming an addictive distraction.

The silly things these men keep asking and saying are unbelievable. Just a few more swipes and I'll have reached my daily limit and can drop this nonsense.

Arnold and Jim came out of the stairwell onto the patio in their new black pants and T-shirts. Will looked up from his work, pulling his sunglasses down.

Arnold spread his arms theatrically. "This is more like it. Good ole breaking and entering. By the way, how do we look?"

"Like a couple of Jewish Metallica fans."

The pair made black-leather-gloved devil signs together, banged their heads, and bumped into each other. Still laughing, Jim exited the mosh pit and stepped over to Will.

"How's it going, boss? We're dressed right and ready. Any word about our mystery men?"

"I've been searching the local internet dating sites hoping to see one of them—strikeout there." Will's phone vibrated; he picked it up, read the reply, and said, "We've got our answer; headquarters confirmed the men in the pictures are Quds Force. The rental car contract is in the name of a guy named Pedro Gonzalez." He looked up with a raised eyebrow.

Will presented the picture on his phone, and the other two leaned in for a closer look. The driver's license photo showed a Hispanic-looking man with similar features to their mystery men. Likely made using a stolen identity.

"Well, he could've rented it and sent these two to spy on Hedyeh for something completely unrelated to our mission."

Will looked up at Arnold. "That's true. I hadn't considered that angle. Who knows what Hedyeh has been up to here? However, nothing in the background checks indicate he's up to anything nefarious. We'll keep it in mind moving forward, and I'll order a deeper background check on Hedyeh."

"Okay, so what else do we need to be doing?"

"Well, the truck is ready. We won't fill up the blimp until around six this evening, so—" He glanced at his watch. "It's 1:30 now. I think we're ready as far as the complicated stuff goes. Free-time until showtime."

Arnold and Jim grinned like wolves.

"I'm not even going to ask what that's about."

The two men fist-bumped. Jim said, "We'll be back in a few hours." They hurried back downstairs.

"Okay, just be back by five," Will said after them.

"Roger that," they said.

Will contemplated the actual takedown. *People are unpredictable and will do crazy things for freedom. Like have a hidden weapon or have friends show up unexpectedly while we're in the middle of seizing him.*

He scanned a drawing of the office complex, making a few notes.

Adjacent to the building is an identical one. This unit is where Henry and I park the truck. We'll let Arnold and Jim out over here between the buildings and pull around like so. He ran a finger from the back of Hedyeh's place to the nearby building.

He returned his finger to the back door. *From the truck, we'll monitor and wait for the signal to bring it around for pickup.* He tapped on the rear entrance before running his finger over to the neighboring building.

Yvette can park at the loading docks across the lot. In the van, John will have over watch, following us after we launch. Kevin will deploy a cat, assuming we get one functional. I'll have him scout the area, and we'll stagger the arrivals. Blimp first, Yvette and the cat second. We'll drop the grab team and post up with the big truck back here. Give them, say, five minutes between arrivals. Arnold and Jim will pick the lock, enter the building, and capture the doctor. We come around, pick them up, and we're out of there. If all is clear, retrieve the cat and depart.

Gabby came to mind. He missed her intensely. She got overshadowed by the preparation and stress. Right now, he wished he could call her before they went out. Picking up his phone, he brought up the number pad and dialed her number. About to hit 'call,' he paused with his thumb over the button. *Come on, you know better. Stay focused. After tonight, you'll probably be on your way home to her, anyway. If all goes well, I'll sneak in a quick unauthorized call late tonight.*

He quit the phone app, set his phone down, and closed his laptop. *It's hot, and I'm thirsty, and I need to relax. I need to get my mind off things. And a beer sounds good.*

Henry stepped out onto the patio. "Uh, Will, I wanted to talk to you alone for a second."

"Sure, what do you need?"

"Nothing I need or want." Henry pulled out a chair and sat in it. "Except to say to you that there's nothing wrong with taking our time. And I don't mean to be stepping on your toes or anything."

Why would he say something like this to me? I've got this and don't need a second-guessing. "I think things are going rather nicely. The time it takes to complete a mission is important. What if Nafisi gets nabbed tonight because we don't act? Or we have a more serious encounter with Quds Force?"

Henry heaved a sigh at the young man's bravado. "Those are all valid points. If we miss the target tonight, we miss the target. There will be other opportunities. In our line of work, we tend to fly by the seat of our pants, anyway. I'd be remiss if I didn't advise you from experience. Things rushed encounter more—problems."

"Then we'll deal with them. That's another part of what we do: adaptability. We're all trained and skilled, or we wouldn't be here. Do you seriously think this is too much for us to handle?"

"No, no, nothing like that. I'm a little more methodical. Maybe it's just from being embedded for so long. Always thinking long-term. As I said, I just wanted to get it off my chest and offer some friendly advice."

Will knew Henry had the best intentions. It still annoyed him to be second-guessed. His temper didn't get the best of him this time, though. "How about this? We'll be extra mindful of the situation tonight. We won't take any sign of trouble for granted. Will that sit better with you?"

Henry heaved a sigh again and smiled warmly at Will. "I'm on board with everything and tonight's mission. You're right—we're all good at this and will complete yet another successful mission. Speaking of which, Kevin has the broken cats disassembled downstairs, trying to get one of them going."

XIV

When Will and Henry stepped into the kitchen, everyone except Arnold and Jim were present. Kevin assessed the operability of the cats side by side on the dining room table. Yvette made him put some newspaper on the table where he was working.

"Can't you take those dirty things out to the garage to work on?" Yvette asked.

Kevin poked at a cat. "I would if I had more light out there. But it's dark, and I need good lighting."

She scowled, threw a dishtowel over one shoulder, and folded her arms. "Well, I better not find one scratch on my table."

"I promise I'll be careful, besides—" He flicked a corner of the newspaper with a finger. "—I've got the newspaper down as you asked."

Will asked, "What's the status of our kitty?" Without the fake fur, it looked like a matte-black cat skeleton.

"Ugh, I dunno. I'm just digging out some leaves and grass that got caught up inside. And making sure everything is tight and connected. The damage looks irreparable, though. If we're lucky, I can cannibalize enough parts between the two to make one functional."

"What is it? The pink stuff."

"They wouldn't tell us in training. Classified and all that," Kevin said. "It's some kind of electrically stimulated inorganic material for creating locomotion. I don't have any idea what the material is or how they made it."

Will fulfilled his desire for a beer by getting one from the fridge. He sat down at the operating table and took a swig from a LandShark Lager bottle. The one's crushed pelvis was beyond repair, while the other's smashed head was all pink goo and what looked like white rubber bands bulging from the cracks.

"Can you do a brain transplant?" Will examined the material by picking at a leg. "Will it rot or spoil being exposed like this?"

"I don't know. It's the first time John, or I, have used them in an actual operation. I'm going to swap the head units and cross my fingers."

Kevin set down the mobile unit and stood at the end of the table. He switched a headlight on, strapped it to his head, and brought out a pair of fourteen-centimeter forceps from his back pocket.

"As I said, they don't tell us the hows and whys, just what it does."

He picked at the edge of some 'fur' with forceps until he had a solid grip to peel it away. It opened like a hatch, revealing white meat marinating in a pink gel.

Leaning in close to the exposed gore, Kevin said, "It doesn't smell. There's no change in its odor that I can detect since it got exposed to air."

Yvette came over to listen in and find out for herself. A minute later, Henry and John were there too. Kevin detached both heads and swapped them. An hour later, it was time to see if surgery was successful.

Using a C-shaped stand, he attached it to the cat using a small ring on its back. It hung limply from the upper end of the C. For control; he used a game controller. He switched the Frankenstein cat on. After an interminable boot sequence, it finally came alive.

"I've turned on its internal overrides because I'm getting error codes all over the place. Some things aren't working right after the transplant. Also, I have it dangling, so it doesn't go wild on us. We should be able to make those 'muscles' work now."

Kevin picked up his controller. The cat jerked and came alive, its limbs making slow, probing movements, searching for traction on a non-existent ground. He gave a gentle nudge. A back leg twitched, then the other. Before their eyes, the cat animated, pawing at the air.

"Hell yeah! Arnold's fat ass and a terrorist couldn't keep our cat down," Kevin said with a fist pump. "I assumed we could repair them." He shrugged. "Never tried it. When I went to see about ordering parts for this one, the order got denied. And they want the cat's back immediately after the mission."

"I think they're creepy," Yvette said.

John said, "It's top-secret stuff. I'm not surprised they're irreplaceable." He clucked his tongue. "That was some perfect timing, body-slamming Arnold right as the cat went by."

Kevin snorted. "Yeah, well, he had it coming. Like any other kid, I got bullied sometimes in school. My uncle made sure I learned jujitsu, and I stopped getting harassed by anybody. Arnold is a bully, whether or not he knows it."

"You sound like such a whiny girl when you say bully," Yvette said. "He's an ass. Just say it like it is— an ass"

Kevin chuckled. "A whiny girl? Sure, I can call him an ass. He's an ass. That was easy." He smiled at Yvette.

"That's better." She came over and put her hands on Kevin's shoulders. "A jackass senses people they can pick on. A grown man, calling another grown man a 'bully' screams, 'pick on me.' So, don't do that."

"Yes, ma'am. No more saying bully. It's ass from here on out."

Will laughed, relieved to feel his mind loosening up a little. They're close to the prize. The mission felt all but completed. The Mossad crew remained in the kitchen around the table for the next couple of hours, hemming and hawing about everything from politics to robots taking all the jobs. He regretted that Jim and Arnold didn't join the bonding session, as they went to a pub instead of hanging around the house. He figured everybody needed a little downtime, anyway.

XV

Standing on the rooftop patio, Will watched an overcast sky. Winds had picked up significantly. Weather reports expected these windy conditions throughout the night. As if in response, a gust whipped at his hair. He checked his watch: 6:05 pm.

Overwatch using the blimp is too risky now, especially with a cat on board. It's possible the brothers may leave before we even arrive. In that scenario, we'd need to give it another shot tomorrow.

By 8:30pm, the blimp would've been set up, inflated, and ready. It didn't matter now. Disappointed, he turned back inside and down the narrow stairway. He stepped off the stairs into the dining room, where everyone gathered.

"It's way too windy. No over watch for tonight's mission."

Arnold said, "Good. One less gizmo to glitch on us. Two less."

"That sucks," John said,pointing a thumb at Kevin. "I guess we'll double up on the cat. I can do the extra stuff like hacking the Wi-Fi or whatever."

Kevin said, "Yeah, that'll make driving easier on me."

"All right," Will said, glancing down at his notepad. "Yvette, you three will take the minivan."

Will leaned on the dining room table, spreading out a hand-drawn map of the office park. He marked the map earlier using a red Sharpie marker. His finger landed directly across from Hedyeh's back door, indicated by a red-circled 'X.'

"The warehouse across from theirs gets quiet soon after 5:00pm. Workers in the vicinity exit the complex within fifteen minutes past five from what we've observed. You'll can park here and run surveillance with no hassles. If someone is present when we arrive, or after we're in position, we'll try to wait them out and hope they leave quickly. If not, your alternate spot will be here." He pointed to an adjacent building marked X-Alt.

"If you must move, here's where you'll go. There's a dumpster in the middle. It'll give you something to do if you have to act like you're supposed to be there—like throw away a box or something. You three will also provide backup support for Arnold and Jim in case they have problems inside. Standard arms tonight—non-Israeli, suppressed semi-autos."

Henry quietly stepped out of the room and returned carrying a sizeable red-and-white cooler. It looked hefty, judging by the way he moved it past them. He set it on the floor and flipped it open.

A row of five Glock 19, 9mm pistols, barrels embedded in black foam, nestled with grips protruding. Screw-on suppressors stood in a second row like cigars. Henry pulled a gun out of the cooler and held it up. "These have all had their serial numbers ground off. So don't get caught by the authorities with one. You can clean them and throw them away if you have to do so."

He reached back into the cooler, brought out a suppressor, and threaded it onto the pistol. Henry stepped out of the way. The others rose and armed themselves.

When Henry finished assembling his gun, he held it aloft. "You don't screw it on with a lot of force. Finger-tight is good enough. There, now you've had your training session. Questions?"

The group chortled at the brevity of his 'training' session, which is how field operators like it: short and sweet.

Kevin said, "These are nice guns." He held open the slide, inspecting the hardware. "Too bad we can't keep them. I've seen lots of YouTube videos about Glock nineteens. Trendy gun."

As Arnold scooped up a box of hollow-points from the cooler, he said, "These are, indeed, some smooth lead slingers. Not much stopping power, though." He spun his Glock around on a forefinger before dropping it into an imaginary holster at his hip.

"Let's all make sure we keep track of these and get them back." Will said, while pressing bullets into a magazine. "Arnold and Jim, you're going to be the only ones who must draw their weapons, anyway. The rest of you treat this location as a public place where we wouldn't want a brandished gun seen. I've got a fanny pack for mine."

Arnold guffawed. "I can't believe you admit to owning a fanny pack."

"Hey, it does the job." Will tugged at the fanny pack's buckle and cleared his throat. "So this brings us to the truck. Once Yvette is in place, she'll give us the all-clear. We'll come in through the main driveway." He stopped loading bullets and pointed at the map. "And stop here to let you out."

Now he dragged his finger to the minivan's spot. Yvette stepped closer, eyed the map, and gave a quick nod.

"We should see you and vice versa as we pass by. Once they're out, we'll continue further back to the next lot and monitor things from there."

Arnold, rubbing at his chin, said, "The back door may or may not be locked. I'm guessing they would've opened it if they took delivery. It's likely to be unlocked. Either way, I'm an expert lock picker. It'll take me less than a minute to crack it."

Jim gave Arnold a dubious face, then said, "Based on floor plans I found on a real estate website, it should be just a warehouse in the back and an office area up front. How come we never looked inside this place? We're going in kind of blind. I'm not worried; it's just two old men. Still—"

"We just don't have time to break in and do proper reconnoitering now that the timeline got pushed up, thanks to those agents snooping around," Will said. "We can't pass on this easy opportunity. If tonight's mission gets scrubbed, we'll consider breaking in and lying in wait next time."

Arnold said, "Okay, so we get inside, nab Nafisi, and drag him out back."

"Yes, tell us you've got him, and we'll pull around with the truck so you can load him inside. Incapacitate the good doctor using zip ties. Yvette, when you hear they've got him, that's your cue to leave the premises."

"Got it. And we come straight back to the house?" she asked.

"No. Go to the farm with everybody else."

"What? Why?"

"Because I want plenty of security around this man. Once he's settled in, we can relax and separate."

Yvette heaved a sigh and folded her arms, but didn't protest any further. Will turned back to the others.

"Once we've got him secured, we'll contact the institute and arrange his extraction. It's up to Tel Aviv after that. We can wrap this mission up in record time. Maybe we can get out of here by the end of the week."

"And maybe you'll relax and let us enjoy ourselves here in beautiful Charleston," Arnold said.

Will smiled. "Yes, I promise we can get out of Yvette's house and have the liberty to do as we please. Only after Nafisi is in custody and secure at the safe house. We'll have to set up a watch schedule, depending on how long it takes to get him shipped out."

"Finally," Arnold said, raising his hands to the heavens. "This hasn't been a fun trip. I've only talked to women in cyberspace. And we've done nothing except go to a local pub for a couple of hours. Usually, there's a long buildup to things, and we have time for other activities. Like it or not, things have jumped straight to showtime. I kind of like your efficient style, Mr. Will." He rubbed his hands together, turning to leave. "Come on, Jim, let's get changed and ready. I want to do some rehearsal in the garage."

"Sounds good to me," Jim said and left with him.

Two hours later, Arnold and Jim rode in the truck's back with Henry at the wheel. Will rode shotgun. Yvette and the others had a ten-minute head start. When they arrived, they saw the office lights still illuminated. The Nafisi brothers worked into the evening.

Kevin reported the cat deployed and had seen nothing interesting. He'd posted it in some bushes for the time being. The back door and entire back lot were visible from that vantage point. With everything in place, Henry stopped the truck at the building's corner.

"Okay, guys. This is where you get off," Will said into his Bluetooth earbuds.

"All right, here we go," Arnold said.

The back door of the truck slid up with a rattle and closed with a thump.

"Okay, we're clear."

Feeling the pressure and anxiety build, Will nodded to Henry, who drove the truck to its place. When they parked, Will hopped out and immediately lit a smoke. Since his gun is cumbersome with a suppressor attached, he held it in a fanny pack that hung at his front.

What's wrong with a fanny pack, anyway? They're convenient.

Henry stayed in the Isuzu, prepared to move at a moment's notice. Will took a few drags, then walked to the corner of the building and peered around. Leaves swished in the trees around the complex. Arnold's voice came through his earbuds.

"We're at the back door. Working the lock now."

Will moved to the next corner. He noted the minivan was fifty meters away to the left. The silhouettes of Arnold and Jim were at the back door, approximately 50 meters across on the right.

Not a single car had driven through since they'd arrived. A sense of eeriness descended upon the scene, like a hushed woodland.

Movement at the far end of the lot caught his eye. Someone emerged from the shadows and headed towards the minivan. "Yvette. Guys. Somebody is coming. Don't do anything yet—he may just be passing by." He prepared to run back to the truck if this person kept coming.

Yvette said, "I see him. He's walking straight towards us. What the hell do you think he wants?"

Will peeked around the corner. The person approaching had disappeared. He couldn't see him on the other side of the van. Through his earbuds, the sliding door opened on the minivan.

A man yelled in the background.

Yvette screamed.

The next sounds made his blood run cold.

Kevin said, "Shoot him!"

THUD THUD THUD THUD THUD

XVI

The suppressed submachine gun fire was unmistakable. "Yvette! Kevin! John! What happened?" All Will got in response were gurgling noises and moaning. He broke into a sprint toward the minivan, fumbling with the zipper on his fanny pack.

Arnold said, "We cracked the lock. What was that? Should we—"

"Keep going. Be careful. Henry, something just—"

"I heard. Yvette! Answer dammit!"

Through their earpieces, they heard Kevin. "My eye!"

A male voice spoke Persian in the background. "Who are you? What are you doing here? Answer me!"

"My eye!"

Again, Arnold asked, "What's going on?"

Will heard Henry start the truck as he crouched behind the van. The man's shoes scratched on the pavement. His muffled voice made Will's heart skip a beat. He saw the man's feet under the minivan. As he peered around at the side door, he saw the legs connected to the feet, leaning into the van at the sliding door.

Will rose and stepped out into a shooting stance, bringing his pistol to bear. "Don't move!"

The man whipped around, his eyes gleaming white saucers against his tan features. His submachine gun moved toward Will. A split second to react.

POP POP

The man's head snapped back. He collapsed like a wet sack into the open door, blood pouring from the two new holes in his head. Though suppressed, Will's pistol still seemed loud as hell relative to the quiet all around them.

He dove for the door, shoving the man away. Yvette's slumped position against the window, with a bloody hole in her head, filled him with horror. Bullet holes lined the windshield and driver's door window.

John didn't move or make a sound in the front seat. Bullet holes puckered the back of it. Will's stomach lurched and threatened to eject its contents. He forced himself to check the back seat.

Kevin, slumped over in the shadows, looked dead.

Please no.

The young agent moaned. Will reached and hauled him upright. The junior agent rose, both hands clutching his bloodied head. His VR goggles had a hole in one side and sat cockeyed on his head.

"Ah! Will, he shot me in the eye! I can't see! Fuck, it hurts! Yvette tried to draw on him, but he got her. He got her, Will! Fuck, I saw it all. I couldn't get my goggles off in time. I couldn't stop him."

He winced and leaned forward as his wound throbbed. Will surveyed the bullet holes in the rear window behind Kevin. His right eye was a bloody mess; a single bullet caught him. Kevin had been fortunate. The slug passed through the edge of his VR goggles, hit his eye socket at an angle, and destroyed his right eye. Narrowly missing his brain.

He should live. But the others. Oh, my God!

"Get down!" Arnold said through his earbuds.

Will reflexively flinched.

THUD THUD THUD THUD THUD THUD THUD

He pulled out of the van and dropped into a crouch. He looked at the closed door where Arnold and Jim had just gone through, but there was nothing else to see.

POP POP POP POP POP POP

The return fire sent Will running for the back door.

THUD THUD THUD

"Arnold! What's the situation?"

POP POP POP POP

"Henry! Get around here now! They're all down!"

Already on the move, Henry said, "On my way. Yvette! Say something! Anybody!"

THUD THUD THUD THUD THUD

More shots from inside. The image of Yvette's corpse flashed in Will's mind. He swallowed the knot forming in his throat. Hope kept him going. *Maybe her wounds looked worse than they were. And John, Christ! I didn't even look at him. What the hell is going on?*

"Kevin's severely injured." He left out the part about Yvette. "Hurry! I just heard more shots inside. I'm checking."

He slammed against the wall next to the closed door, gulped in air, checked his weapon, and swallowed. Cracking the door, inside it's dark. Opening it a little further, he saw light spilling through a doorway in the far wall.

The odor of cordite wafted out at him. He slid through and took up a crouching position behind some plastic-wrapped copy machines. Silence, at first, then raised voices speaking in Persian echoed farther away in the building.

"They're Jews! Look at them. Probably Mossad; who else would be here?" A man said. "The FBI would've sent professionals, not these amateurs."

"Where's Saeed?" Another male voice said.

"He said he was going to look at that vehicle outback. It's been a few minutes."

Will checked his pistol again before scrambling through the menagerie of plastic-wrapped machines.

Up ahead, through the doorway, he saw a pair of motionless legs lying inside on the floor.

He couldn't tell whose they were. Moving closer, he reached the doorway and looked around the corner. Will saw Arnold and Jim splayed out on the office floor, pools of blood growing under them. Jim wasn't moving. Arnold was clutching a leg. A man with a submachine gun squatted next to them, eyeing Arnold and rifling through Jim's pockets.

Enraged, Will stood from his hiding place and drew a bead on the man. "Don't move!"

Startled, the man fell backward as he twisted to meet Will. Again, Will didn't hesitate.

POP POP

Two shots to the man's head dropped him instantly to the floor. Will rushed forward before someone else came out of nowhere. Arnold moaned and lifted his head. They made eye contact, and Will held a finger to his lips.

"Who's there? Mahmud? Answer me!" A man said from further away in the office.

Bright-red blood soaked Arnold's pant leg. Will grabbed Arnold's hand and pressed it against the wound. They made eye contact. He nodded at Arnold, who bobbed his head weakly, knowing his wounded leg was severe. Will's only hope was taking these assholes out and getting him medical attention. He moved deeper inside the office.

Boxes and machines haphazardly cluttered the whole place. In the front office's window, he saw the reflection of three people standing in the cluttered front area. Hedyeh stood to the left, Vahan center, and a third man peeking over a cubicle wall. Will saw his gun trained on the brothers. He also recognized him from the Yorktown. A wave of fresh anger washed over him.

Will glanced at his teammates before he came around the corner, pistol raised. "Don't move! Drop your weapon!"

The man's eyes narrowed. He recognized Will too.

"Who are you?" Will said in Persian.

"Who are you?" the man said, stepping out some from the cubicle.

"Drop your weapon!"

"Who are you?" The man said, scowling and tightening his grip on his gun.

Will stepped forward. "Drop it! I won't harm you if you put down your gun."

Hedyeh whimpered and said, "Please, don't hurt us. We've done nothing. We only want peace."

The man glared at Hedyeh, moving closer to him. "Shut your cowardly mouth! I should shoot you right now. My place in heaven is secure. Is yours?" He gazed at the ceiling. "Allah, I commend my spirit to you. Let me take these infidels with me!" He raised his gun.

Will squeezed his trigger.

POP

The man's head jerked, releasing a pink spray with a flap of skin. Stunned, but not incapacitated by the grazing bullet, he renewed his motion to execute the brothers. Will aimed lower.

POP POP

Two red spots appeared on the left breast of the man's white button-down shirt. He grimaced, clutched at his wound, and menaced the cringing brothers. Submachine gun coming to bear in shaking hands.

"No!" Will said, lunging forward.

"Vahan!" Hedyeh said, stepping in front of his brother. They raised their futile hands.

THUD THUD THUD THUD THUD

Will couldn't tell if they'd gotten hit as they fell to the floor. The Persian man collapsed in a heap. He stood frozen, holding his pistol at the ready, momentarily unable to process the last few minutes. Things had taken such a horrible turn in such a short period.

Outside, Henry leaped from the truck and ran to the minivan driver's door. He flung it open, catching Yvette's lifeless body before it fell out. Gently pushing her back in, he recoiled from the carnage, putting a fist in his mouth as tears welled up. "Oh, Yvette, Yvette, Yvette! She's dead, Will! They killed her!" He rushed to John, feeling for a pulse on his neck. "John's gone, too."

Kevin's weak voice came over the net. "Yvette, John —"

Remembering his wounded comrades, Will spun and ran back to check on Arnold and Jim. He turned his phone's flashlight on to examine them. Pale and sweating profusely, Arnold remained conscious. He'd found a bungee cord and used it as a tourniquet around his upper thigh. Breathing hard and ragged, he had nothing to say—excruciating pain will silence even a man like him.

Will, looking at Jim, grimaced. The 9mm hole in his head was obviously fatal. Never mind the amount of blood loss. He was gone. *Dammit! Fuck, I'm sorry, Jim.*

He turned back toward the brothers. Vahan Nafisi was rising from the floor. Relieved, Will stood and raised his pistol.

"Hedyeh!" Vahan cried, bending over his brother. "Hedyeh!"

Vahan Nafisi's brother, Hedyeh, lay motionless on the floor. In his dying act, the Quds Force agent had shot the wrong man.

"Hedyeh!" Nafisi said with a wail.

"Son of a bitch. They got Jim too, Henry. I think they hit Hedyeh." Will moved to Arnold. "Arnold, speak to me."

A groggy Arnold said, "The bastards got me in the leg. Lots of blood—" With his tourniquet tightened, his eyes fluttered and rolled up; He lost consciousness, flopping onto his back.

XVII

Footsteps behind Will made him whirl, gun aimed.

"Will? It's me! Don't shoot," Henry said, hands up.

Will relaxed, pointing his gun toward the ceiling. "Sorry. I'm—sorry. I'm so sorry about Yvette. Is John —"

Henry didn't respond as he surveyed the room. The pools of blood stopped growing when hearts stopped pumping and spirits left bodies.

"Yes, John and Yvette—are no longer with us," Henry said as he knelt by Jim and Arnold, hand over mouth. "Oh, Jim. Dammit, Will, they got him, too. What a terrible night." He bow his head for a quick prayer.

The two men pondered their next move in silence for a few seconds. Henry drummed his fingers on his lips until he noticed Arnold's injury. "He's still alive, but looks to have lost a lot of blood. Arnold. Arnold, can you hear me?" He tapped the unconscious agent on the cheek a few times.

Arnold groaned.

Will snapped out of his shock and rushed over. Arnold passed out from blood loss. Fortunately, his wound was dark red crusty clot, thanks to his tourniquet and pants. No blood gushing out. Henry found a roll of paper towels, handing it to Will over his shoulder. He unrolled ten sheets and folded them into a pad. Henry squatted next to him and held the pad in place on Arnold's leg while Will made a couple more. A few wraps of packing tape and they had him ready for transport.

"They arrived from the front shortly after we did? I don't know. Maybe they were already here. Is Kevin okay?" Jim's words echoed in his head about why they hadn't broken into the office beforehand. *Why didn't I listen? Why was I in such a rush?*

"I gave Kevin a towel to hold on his head," Henry said.

Will quickly checked the entire office and found it empty. Out front, the rental Chevy Cruze from the night before sat. Arnold seemed stable for the moment. Henry grabbed a few paper towels and went out to the car.

Meanwhile, Will ran out to the minivan. He tended to Kevin, chucking the dirty towel and applying a paper towel bandage to his eye and comforting him as best he could. With apprehension, he kept watch, fearing security guards or the police would show up.

Henry found little in the Cruze. A couple of duffel bags with nothing except clothing and several 9mm ammunition boxes inside. He searched for witnesses but saw nobody. Using the paper towels, he wiped the car's interior for prints. After completing his quick wipe down, he went back inside.

Will came back inside too. "Kevin will lose an eye and it's my fault. We should've waited. I should've been more cautious."

Henry, hearing Will's shock, hesitated before speaking. "Nothing important in the car, boss. We need to get this cleaned up."

Will turned to Henry with a deep scowl creasing his face. "Your wife was just murdered. Aren't you the least bit upset?"

Henry heaved a long sigh, which was becoming habitual. "We don't have time for this. But if it'll help; we're colleagues, content to serve Israel and pursue our interests. It wasn't a relationship of love. It greatly saddens me, none the less. I'll explain later."

Henry's voice sounded distant to Will. *Can I even trust my own thoughts?* "I'm sorry. I'm—I don't know what I think right now."

"Take some deep breaths. You're in a little shock. It's okay, I understand. Believe me; the night is only beginning. We'll call in a cleaner now. This place needs sanitizing, but first, we must move the bodies before somebody shows up."

Incredulous, Will spun around, pondering Sgt. Cohen's possible reaction. *What would he have said about all this?* They trained for this, but practice couldn't imbue the psychological impact. He stopped in front of Henry.

"Move them?" Will's tone became sarcastic as he said, "Yes, of course. Here are three dead people who were walking and talking to us just a few minutes ago. It's a little traumatizing to me at the moment." Will dug both hands into his hair, closed his eyes, and held the pose for a moment.

Henry stepped close to Will, reached out, and gently gripped his upper arm. "I know. You must calm yourself. Who else is going to do it? These kinds of contingencies are what I train to do. It is what Yvette and I do." His voice caught. "Did."

Will lowered his arms. Henry looked earnestly into his wide eyes and trying to calm him through their locked gaze. Genuine tears threaten overflowing the edges of Henry's eyes.

After a moment, Henry broke the silence. "Now," he sniffed. "We'll have to put the bodies in the truck. By the time we get done, the cleaners should be here. They'll cover up the scene. I'll drive the truck. You must drive the van with Kevin."

Will grimaced, thinking about the blood and gore from Yvette and John in the front seats. *What has happened? What has this night turned into? Am I going to wake up from this nightmare?*

They loaded their dead comrades into the truck, one by one. Placing them respectfully inside near the cab end. The three Iranian agents got piled together with Hedyeh at the Isuzu truck's back door. Before they put them in, they photographed, fingerprinted, and collected DNA from each man using kits Henry brought.

Dr. Nafisi, utterly distraught and shocked, waxed silent and catatonic, making it easy to handle him. They ushered him into the Isuzu front seat with little effort, zip tying one wrist to the door.

Kevin stayed in the van.

While walking through the office one last time, the cleaners showed up. Henry greeted them, then ushered them back. A black man, looking thoroughly gangsta, strutted inside. The man wore pants hung low on his hips, a cocked ball cap, sunglasses (even at night), and a street swagger. Behind him, two Asian women followed as if ready to clean hotel rooms. They had two carts loaded with cleaning supplies and expressionless faces.

Will left out the back.

"Thank you for coming so quickly."

"Yeah, yeah, no prob. You always pay good, so I like taking care of my best customers, yo. What'cha got tonight?"

"Oyvey, it's a mess," Henry said, pressing a hand to his forehead as he turned toward the office interior.

The cleaner pulled down his shades. "Gyatdam! Y'all made a muthafuck'n mess!"

"Yes, a tragic ambush. Give it the usual treatment. No prints, hair, or DNA."

"Don't worry, I got you, dawg. No worries, ya feel me? The girls and me'll have this shit scrubbed in an hour. Nobody'll know anything happened."

Will retrieved the cat from the bushes. He waited out back, smoking a cigarette, cat under an arm. Losing three agents in seconds was beyond his training expectations. *Maybe in a war, but not like this.* A new sense of paranoia gripped him, and he wanted to leave. Now.

The van was a wretched mess. He used a small blue tarp donated by the Nafisi's to cover the seat. It took a minute to collect himself before climbing inside. *At least the shivering has stopped.* The adrenaline letdown always gave him a chill.

Henry emerged from the back and promptly gestured for a smoke. Will obliged.

"Follow me to the funeral home. It's not too far from here. They'll give our brothers and sisters the proper honors they deserve. Some others will be there to tend to Arnold and Kevin." He lit the cigarette and took a long drag.

"A convenient asset, the funeral home. What're they going to do with the Iranians?"

Henry exhaled his smoke. "Our network is extensive here in America. Many operations overlap other operations. These sorry bastards will get taken care of quickly."

Will closed his eyes and rubbed at his neck. *The whole mission is shit! They're dead, and I'm left to go down in flames after they investigate this debacle. What the fuck happened tonight? What the fuck?*

"Hey, Will, or whatever your name is, are you okay? You look a little ill," Henry asked, wagging his cigarette pinched between two fingers.

"Yes, I'm just a little—disturbed is all. You're taking this all in stride. How do you do it?"

"Long ago, I dedicated my life to serving Israel in this manner. Maybe that sounds trite, but that's how I see it. Since then, I've seen a lot of terrible things. It's something you need to come to terms with yourself. I mean, truly in your heart. We must remain strong and fix the mishaps. They happen, son. Count yourself lucky that you're still breathing. That was some quick shooting you did. I'm not sure I would've been able to do that."

Not feeling incredibly proud, Will opened the van door. "Have they got things here? What about the car?"

"I found the car keys in one of these guys' pockets and gave them to the cleaner. They'll take care of it all. In an hour, nobody will figure out what happened. And we'll be long gone."

Will nodded, tossing the cat onto the passenger seat as he slid onto the driver's side. The blue plastic tarp crackled, feeling cold through his pant legs. He closed the door, lit up another cigarette, and started the engine while Henry got the truck going.

Jim, John, Yvette. Guys, I'm sorry. I should've been more careful. We should have kept a closer watch at the front. So many things that are so obvious now. "Fuck!"

Will pressed both palms hard to his eyes, letting off after a few seconds. The truck pulled away; he put the van in gear and followed.

Fifteen minutes of driving to the funeral home made him nauseous. The stink of blood curdled Will's stomach. Kevin's moans of pain didn't help matters. Even cigarettes were making him sick. When they arrived at the funeral home, an older man wearing black pants, a white shirt, and a black-tie met them.

"Good evening, gentlemen," Ismail Monash said. "I hear you've had a bit of tragedy."

Henry replied, "Shalom Ismail. Tragedy is an understatement. We got ambushed. Quds Force."

Ismail's thick eyebrows rose. "Oh my, this is news to me. I didn't know they were operating in America." He glanced around, as if expecting to catch someone lurking.

"Nobody did; they followed our mark sooner and more intensely than we expected."

"Ah, I'm sorry to hear that. Somebody's head will roll, I'm sure. Such a tragedy any time one of our heroes falls." He clucked his tongue. "Let's get them inside."

They unloaded the bodies. Placing Jim, Yvette, and John on gurneys. Ismail held a brief service for them that Henry and Will attended before leaving.

Ismail called them "brothers and sisters—heroes of Israel" at the brief memorial. Meanwhile, Hedyeh and the Quds Force men went to the crematory. Henry had his work cut out, normalizing his secret life with his wife's sudden disappearance.

Will had to write a detailed report and catch a long flight to Nuremberg in the morning. The Institute made the arrangements as soon as they gave their preliminary accounts. He'd have to explain what happened and why to his superiors. Before now, he'd always envisioned receiving a medal or award for his heroics.

This, though. What is this? Did we succeed or fail? Six lives for one.

Two women and a middle-aged man dressed in civilian clothes came and tended to Arnold and Kevin. When the medics got them stabilized, they loaded into unmarked vans and departed. Destination unknown to Will or Henry. Henry would take care of Dr. Nafisi at the safe house. When all was said and done, it left nothing to do besides leaving Charleston.

XVIII

Will was uncertain of ever seeing the others again. Keeping in touch would be dangerous. Three Mossad agents are dead. Paying hell is what he expected. On the way to the airport, Henry explained himself more.

"Yvette is my third Mossad wife, you know."

"No, shit. What happened to the other two? Not a similar fate, I hope."

"My first wife contracted cancer and died three years into our cover here. The second wife they sent me lasted for a couple of years; she resigned and went back to Israel. I guess I didn't do it for her. Yvette and I, we've been paired for fourteen years." Henry scratched at his beard. "This sounds terrible, but a replacement wife is probably in the works already. And my replacement too, for that matter, in the event something happened to me. The new one will be on her way in a few months, I'm sure."

Will shook his head. "We're expendable. I'll not forget that or them. I won't forget anybody from now on. Our lives are going to matter, even if it's just between us."

"That's why they give out posthumous medals and the like. Yvette and the others will never be forgotten. Their names will go on the wall of the fallen at the institute. Ultimately, God is welcoming them into heaven, so they're in a better place."

"No, I mean personally. I don't give a fuck what the Mossad does. The thought that they'll just be forgotten casualties is so damned screwed up. Their lives must have meaning for the rest of us to go on. Where's Nafisi?"

"You're right there, and with time, you'll heal and understand. Nafisi is secure in the safe house. I've got some friends watching him." Henry didn't say anymore because he knew it was pointless. He agreed with Will. He had nothing to offer for comfort.

At the airport departure curb, Henry stopped the car, put it in park, and got out to help. After Will retrieved his suitcases from the trunk, Henry caught him by surprise at the curb and gave him an unexpected bear hug. "Take care of yourself, Will. I like you," he said with a wide smile.

Will cracked an unexpected smile. "You too, Henry. And it's Karl."

Henry smiled back. "I've used my cover name so long that it's my real name. Ha! They used to call me Zubin before I got into all this spy stuff."

Karl pressed his lips in a tight smile. "I hope we get to work together again sometime, Zubin. We'll drink to the team from Operation: Palmetto. That's assuming they don't dismiss me from the Mossad."

"Nah, you'll have my report to back you up. It'll be fine, kid. We did all we could and tried for the best outcome. Qud's Force surprised us. Bastards! It could've happened to anyone, though. Not to understate the tragedy, mind you."

Karl would never stop feeling like it was his fault they died. He'd carry the burden forever.

Survivor's guilt, I guess. Right now, all I want is to get away from this place.

Will bid Henry one last farewell and watched him drive away. He walked to the smoker's pavilion for a couple of cigarettes. He had some time to spare. To survive the plane ride, a pack of nicotine lozenges in his pocket. It didn't matter that he looked like a fiend. The image of the guy's scalp flipping up made him crave a cigarette. There was nothing that could divert his attention from the scene. The smells and surreal experience of loading and unloading bodies made him want to shower again and again.

Christ! I killed three people within minutes of each other. Six, I count my responsibility to Yvette and them. No amount of training prepares you for that.

Henry had been kind enough to give him a couple of Valium pills from Yvette's stash of prescription medicine. When he got through airport security, he bought bottled water and washed the pills down.

A bar conveniently located across from his gate beckoned. With an hour to kill until his plane took off, Karl drank and eat lozenges. He walked over and ordered two shots of vodka.

Screw the middleman. Just give me alcohol and let me sleep.

His phone vibrated. On looking at the screen, he saw a priority message. He thumbed in and read over the notes. Several piled up while he zoned out, digesting horrific images of death. After he closed the last unread message, the Israeli Cyber Security Directorate took control of his phone, downloaded its data, and wiped it clean. He was too sleepy to be concerned about his phone when he boarded the plane. His brain finally let go of murder and bloody thoughts.

Hours later, a jarring bump onto the runway at Nuremberg International startled him awake. A moment of confusion before he knew which way was up. Drool dripped out of the corner of his mouth and onto his shirt. The man sitting next to him smiled when he glanced his way.

In German, the man said, "Good morning, sunshine. My, you've slept the entire flight. I'm jealous."

Karl raised an eyebrow and found he couldn't make his vocal cords work yet. A tiny bottle of water protruded from the seat pocket. He snatched it out and gulped it down. His bladder responded by alerting him it was reaching critical mass. "How long?" he said, voice a croak.

His first-class seatmate said, "Oh, we've been in the air after our last layover for about eight hours. You came around for a second when we landed after the first leg."

Karl rubbed at his face, sitting up straight. His neck ached, and one of his feet tingled from falling asleep. *Gabby. I'm almost home.*

The rest and some geographical distance rejuvenated his spirits. After debarking the plane, he dashed straight into a men's room. He walked through the terminal rather than riding the tram to baggage claim, hoping to revive himself with the exercise.

Along the way, he picked up a coffee, which he drank as he sucked on a nicotine lozenge. Luggage retrieved, he turned to leave the airport and get a ride home and about knocked Gabriella over. She stood there, smiling. Pure and safe. Ecstatic to have him home.

Why is she here? How did she know when I'd be here? Has something happened? "Gabby!"

"Surprise! I couldn't wait to see you."

"I'm so glad to see you." He dropped his luggage. "How did you know when I'd be here?"

She wrapped her arms around him. He responded in kind, squeezing her tightly.

Whispering in his ear, she said, "Your colleague, Hiram. He said you had a rough trip and would need me to come to get you."

She pushed back from him, looking into his eyes. Deep concern creased her face at the sight of him. Karl's joy faltered briefly as his inner agony seeped out upon seeing her. His smile quivered; he bit his lip and looked down. A tsunami of pain surged to escape. Gabriella hugged him again.

A man to their left suddenly yelled in Persian. "There he is!"

Karl broke their hug and stepped protectively in front of Gabriella. The man was accompanied by a woman and two teenagers. Ten meters in front of them, a slim, bearded man strolled, smiling, with arms outstretched. The woman and teens hugged the man together.

Gabriella's lips touched Karl's ear. "Karl, what's wrong?"

As if coming out of hypnosis, he shook his head and turned to her. He didn't have words. The look of terror combined with embarrassment told her all she needed to know.

"Oh, my darling, say nothing. We can talk later if you want, or if you really want to talk now. It's fine. We should at least go out to the car," she said with a glance around.

He nodded and rubbed his eyes, whispering, "Let's go."

At least it isn't uncommon for sad people to be at the airport. Gabriella grabbed the handle on his rolling suitcase and hooked his arm in hers while he picked up the other suitcase.

"Come on, my love. Let's leave this place and forget about everything else for a while. Okay?"

Karl sniffled and nodded.

Four hours later, he did something agents weren't supposed to do and didn't think he'd ever do: he confessed the complete debacle to Gabriella as they lay in bed. Not the names and details, the overall mission and what happened. She deserved to know what was eating him alive. When he finished, tears were streaming down her cheeks. And he feared he'd made a mistake confiding in her.

"That's awful! I'm so sorry. Karl, we need to get you into a therapist or something tomorrow. You're going to have to take care of this right away. Not because I think you're weak, but just before it eats you up inside. Is it okay to be telling me these things?"

"No. Right now, I don't care. I mean, I care. How could I not tell you enough, so you'd understand? You must swear to keep it all to yourself."

"Of course, I swear."

"I've already been thinking about talking to someone. The Institute will put me in touch with an appropriate shrink. But I'm glad you thought of it, too, so I don't procrastinate. What I want is for my mind to just shut off." He dug his fingers into his scalp and ran them to the back of his neck.

"It's nice out this evening. Let's go walking. The exertion will do you good."

"I don't know. Maybe," he said apathetically. "I'm not exactly tired. I don't feel like doing much of anything."

Gabriella showed him a smile. "All the more reason to go. Let's do it, and then, when we come back, we can lie around and be lazy."

Karl smiled at her and drew her in for a kiss. As they separated, their eyes briefly met. "Thank you for trying to understand. I needed to unload some of this —this garbage."

The pain in his eyes caused her eyes to well up again. She cupped his cheek. "Anything for you, my love."

XIX

A month later, after enduring long and sometimes hostile interviews, Karl finally found himself at a tribunal in Tel Aviv. Judgment on Karl and Operation Palmetto to be rendered.

Thirty days had felt like ninety years to him. The time allowed him to digest things. A few therapy sessions and regular exercise helped. Ultimately, he must independently come to terms with his demons.

The killing hadn't bothered him like losing three members of his team. Their loss stung, but it waned, leaving him with a pang of guilt set on simmer. Nightmares still got him. Waking up drenched in sweat from wild, frantic dreams was down to one or two times a week.

Last night wasn't a good night. And this morning, he sat at the tribunal ready to receive his sentence at the far end of a long cherry wood conference table. The tribunal members' faces are impassive and stern. The middle one had been reading their judgment for some time. As per usual, his palms and pits were sweating from the tension.

Just fucking say it! This guy has been blathering forever. What the hell is going to happen to me?

"All involved," said the tribunal chair, "underestimated the gravity of Dr. Nafisi's departure. They should have taken and used more time and assets to execute this mission. To blame our heroes on the ground for bad intelligence would be a travesty and set a dangerous precedent for other operatives. The tribunal feels you're competent and operational, per your fitness reports. We would be remiss if we deactivated you."

He licked a thumb and flipped the page.

"Leadership is difficult. A trial by fire is the best kind of crucible. Conniving and ruthless enemies know no boundaries. Not all are prepared to cope. Your handling of Operation Palmetto highlighted your inexperience. That is a shortfall on the Mossad's shoulders. Therefore, this tribunal finds Karl Gruben not guilty of negligence and dereliction of duty."

Karl's heavy heart leaped.

"We will mete no punishment out. You are to take a thirty-day sabbatical before returning to duty. At which time, your local handler will contact you and assign you a new task. Additionally, you must complete a training regimen of leadership, tactics, and surveillance courses during the sabbatical. As human beings, we empathize with you and the emotions you must be dealing with after the failure and fallout of Operation Palmetto."

Rub it in, why don't you?

Karl saw his career drowning in red tape. They'd put him out to pasture early and hope he quit and went away. He would continue in remembrance of the Charleston victims. As long as he was able, he wouldn't stop. He'd use this unique position to exact holy revenge on the enemies of Israel. *Not precisely for revenge. To even the score, at least. Maybe. I guess. I don't know. Can I even keep my oaths?*

Operation Palmetto galvanized his commitment and focus. Whatever they handed down, he came prepared to accept it. He expected a harsh punishment. His unexpected, complete vindication caught him off guard. Qud's Force was surfacing more and more. One day, he would have his chance. He knew it.

Revenge it is. I already executed the trigger pullers. Someone directed them to kill my team. That's who I want; the big fish at the top. It might be a mole amongst us. Anywhere I can root them out. When I find the trail, I'm going to follow it until I get to its end.

Figuring out how to identify them was hard enough. They had to be found somewhere in the world. It was daunting. Mossad wasn't interested in his vendetta. Understanding this, he kept his vindictive desire to himself, not even revealing it to Gabby.

The private ax-grinding gave him that bit of purpose he needed. It made sense, given his profession. Living a double life: one as a Mossad agent masquerading as a regular person; and one where he is Karl Gruben, fiance to Gabriella Voss.

Well, now there'd be three lifestyles. Not just two. Mossad, husband, and international vigilante? Mental note: never say 'international vigilante' out loud. It sounds really cheesy.

The tribunal chair cleared his throat, snapping Karl out of his daydreaming. "—in conclusion, we find ourselves left with this lesson: expect the unexpected. The work of the Mossad in its vigilance for Israel's safety is dangerous. Contrary to popular belief, we're not expendable. Each warrior lost costs Israel a fortune in financial damage and irreplaceable human assets."

"As you return to your duties, we pray you will remember these principles and carry them forward to teach the next generation. Please do this, hoping they will not fall prey to a similar tragedy. Thank you all for your time and service. We adjourn this court." The chair banged his gavel on the table and stood. His comrades on the tribunal rose with him.

"All rise!" The bailiff said.

Secret tribunals rarely had a lot of attendees. Karl stood along with everyone else, which included himself and his defense attorney, Jacob Dershowitz. The tribunal and bailiff exited. A few seconds later, the men stood alone.

"Well, that went fantastic. Congratulations. I've seen others pay dearly for less. Your case could have gone either way. Luckily, they saw it for what it was, and you were telling the truth. It's a good day for truth and justice."

He smiled and stuck his hand out to Karl, who grabbed it and gave it a quick shake.

"Thanks for believing in me and seeing this through. I must confess, I'm a little shocked. I don't think I could've prepared so well without you. I guess that's what you're supposed to do."

"All true. Just doing my job. What you said means I did my job right." He glanced at his wristwatch. "Unfortunately, I've got to run. Good luck to you, Karl."

He strode out of the room. Karl walked to a window down the hallway that looked out over Tel Aviv. *Where is Hiram? He said he'd be here.*

Yet another long flight awaited him. After this, he'd go home to recover and mentally prepare for the next assignment. Right now, he felt ready to get back to work. He knew a soft pitch assignment would be best to get his feet wet and confidence restored.

Gabby will want to know the good news.

He dug into his front pants pocket, retrieving his phone.

Karl: Not guilty! A celebration when I get home. I love you. I'll let you know when I'm on the airplane.

Though it's an hours earlier in Nuremberg, she's awake. Less than a minute later, she replied.

Gabby: That's fantastic! Call me when you can. I knew they couldn't burn you. I love you!

He dropped the phone back in his pocket. "Road to recovery—here I come."

Outside the building, Hiram Roth sat in his rental car, cell phone pressed to his ear.

"Of course, I didn't know what they were going to do. The blasted hero acted faster than I could do anything about it. I—"

"Enough!" Said an Asian-accented woman. "Your excuses only aggravate us. Remember your conditioning and promise to help us. Remember what the consequences are for breaking that promise. Imagine your wife and children, toiling in a secret reeducation center. Where you fail, they will attempt to succeed by helping us in whatever capacity we want them to serve. Is that the life you want for them? We could kill them, but where's the benefit of that?"

Hiram closed his eyes tight, pressed a fist to his mouth, and held his breath for a few seconds. As he exhaled, he said, "Of course I don't, and I'm trying to keep my promise. This cluster-fuck was unexpected. Everything was going fine until the team leader got in a hurry."

"If you cannot keep your people under control, we can always find someone else to do it."

Movement coming from the Mossad administration complex caught Hiram's attention. The front doors to the building opened, and Karl Gruben walked out.

"Look, I can't talk right now. I'm keeping my promise. Do you hear me? I'm keeping my bloody damned promise!"

"Our Iranian contacts aren't happy at all about losing another scientist to Israel. You'd better come through next time—no more excuses. There will be things coming that don't involve you. The entire world is going to get swept up into something that will bring it to its knees."

Hiram pulled a face. "What are you talking about?"

"Never mind. Just remember, be ready in Nuremberg. Soon."

The call ended as Karl reached his window, showing a questioning face and outstretched hands.

"Where were you?" Karl asked as the car window came down. "Is everything okay? You look sick."

"Sorry. I got an important phone call that ran long. Some blowhards just love to hear themselves talk, you know? How'd the tribunal go?" Hiram asked with a nervous chuckle.

Karl nodded vacantly. "They exonerated me. Said it was everybody else's fault. I think we've probably got a mole. Can you give me a lift to the airport?"

Hiram gulped. With a forced smile, he said, "Absolutely. Get in."

The end.

Thanks for reading! I hope you enjoyed the story.
Continue through the series with the next
installment. Visit my website so you can sign-up for
my monthly newsletter. --Breach

The Karl Gruben Spy Thriller Series
Operation Palmetto
Operation Palmetto (audiobook)
Operation Watchtower
Operation Blue Eagle
Operation Raven Rock
Operation Snake Oil

Heirs of Judgement Series
Unity Pointe

rtbreach.com